She'd only just m

Alex waved at the sce[...] one of those children's games. I expect the music to stop, and everyone will have to pretend to be statues.'

Lisa giggled. 'Networking,' she explained. Deep inside her she realised she was doing more than enjoy herself at the Blazes Ball. This might—this could—turn into the magic kind of evening she'd been wanting. She knew he was attracted to her. And…

Gill Sanderson is a psychologist who finds time to write only by staying up late at night. Weekends are filled by her hobbies of gardening, running and mountain walking. Her ideas come from her work, from one son who is an oncologist, one son who is a nurse and her daughter who is a trainee midwife. She first wrote articles for learned journals and chapters for a textbook. Then she was encouraged to change to fiction by her husband, who is an established writer of war stories.

A FAMILY
TO SHARE

18

BY
GILL SANDERSON

MILLS & BOON®

For Staff Nurse Delyth Wyn, with many thanks.

First published in Great Britain 1998
Harlequin Mills & Boon Limited,
Eton House, 18-24 Paradise Road, Richmond, Surrey TW9 1SR

© Gill Sanderson 1998

ISBN 0 263 15843 8

Set in Times Roman 11 on 12 pt.
15-9807-49106-D

Printed and bound in Great Britain
by Antony Rowe Ltd, Chippenham, Wiltshire

CHAPTER ONE

SISTER Lisa Grey walked down the centre corridor of
Ward 28, ever-alert blue eyes checking and registering
that all was well. Only occasionally was there excitement on the infectious diseases ward, but today
seemed even quieter than normal.

For the moment Lisa's paperwork was done. She
knew the auxiliaries were preparing beds for new arrivals. Nurse Sarah Rogers was helping the junior
house officer as he checked on old Mr Benson's gastroenteritis. Her other nurse was doing the regular
round, taking each patient's temperature, blood pressure and pulse.

On Ward 28 each patient had his or her own tiny
room and, if she peeped, Lisa could see people reading, listening through headphones or just resting. One
or two with their doors open raised hands in salutation
to the tall red-haired sister, and she waved back.

The afternoon sunshine of early spring shone
through onto the shining floor, illuminating the egg-
shell blue curtains and paintwork. She could even
detect that indefinable hospital smell—a mixture of
food, disinfectant and polish—which acted on her like
a drug whenever she started work. After the first five
minutes it was usually never noticed.

It *was* peaceful.

She could sit in her office, pour herself a coffee
and just relax for five minutes. Then, even as she

thought it, Lisa started a countdown. Ten, nine, eight, seven, six... It never stayed peaceful for that long.

But it did. She was even thinking the unthinkable—had she time for a second mug of coffee? She had—and then the JHO, Dr Paul Evans, and Sarah Rogers joined her.

'I think we've sorted out Mr Benson, Sister,' Paul said, self-importantly. 'When you get on a bit I've learned you must expect the odd ache and pain. Hospitals can't cure everything. I don't think there's anything to worry about.'

'No, Doctor,' Lisa murmured, and exchanged a se-cret amused glance with Sarah. Dr Evans was all of twenty-four years old and, to twenty-eight-year-old Lisa and Sarah—who was over thirty—he seemed in-expressibly young.

He was being more bouncy than usual, more the super-efficient doctor. 'Bleep me if you need me, Sister. I'll drop in again later. Must rush.' Paul drained his coffee mug, and left in a self-satisfied swirl of white coat.

There was a moment's silence, and then Lisa said drily, 'I think you've made a conquest, Sarah. That little show of medical expertise was for your benefit.'

'What?' Sarah was obviously genuinely surprised. Then she smiled. 'Oh, my goodness. He must think I'm an *older woman*! But I still feel young. I don't want a toyboy!'

'Perhaps I should have a cautionary word with him,' Lisa suggested, giggling. 'Advise him about the dangers of women with experience.' This time both of them laughed. They liked Paul, but he was still a bit too conscious of his recently acquired medical di-ploma.

She could also see just how attractive Sarah Rogers was, with her blonde hair, neat figure and a piquant face. Originally Sarah had trained as an SEN—a state enrolled nurse—and had then been persuaded to leave nursing by her new husband. She'd become a hairdresser and beautician. Now she was divorced, had returned to her first love of nursing and was taking a conversion course to become a state registered nurse.

Lisa liked her. She was a hard worker, with a calmness that reassured their patients. But her training as a beautician still showed. Her blonde hair was well shaped, her make-up unobtrusive but effective.

'I'll bet he asks you to dinner later,' Lisa teased. 'What will you say?'

'I'll invite him to come and meet my mother. Say she always wanted me to marry a doctor. That'll frighten him off.'

There was more of the easy laughter of colleagues who knew and trusted each other. Then Sarah asked, 'Is he a good doctor, Lisa?'

Instantly Lisa recognised the warning signs. That was not a fitting question for a nurse to ask. 'He's willing but he's young and inexperienced,' she said cautiously. 'Now, tell me, why did you ask that?' A cynical corner of her mind remembered her countdown. It wasn't peaceful any more.

Sarah was choosing her words with care. 'Well, it may be nothing. You know I've been nursing Mr Benson for the past week?'

'Severe gastroenteritis. He didn't call his GP until he was badly dehydrated and needed a hospital stay because of his age. He's now off his intravenous saline and dextrose. I thought he was doing fine.'

'That's it. He's getting better and he's never complained before, even when things were bad. But now he *is* complaining. He says his shoulder aches. And I wondered…'

'Let's have a look at him.' Lisa put down her coffee-mug. 'It's probably nothing but we can check.'

'I'm sorry to alarm you,' Sarah said as they made their way down the ward. 'I don't want to cause unnecessary trouble.'

Lisa shook her head. 'If you hadn't told me I'd have been upset.'

It didn't take her long to decide that Sarah's suspicions had been correct. Certainly Mr Benson should feel weak, and possibly he might have apparently unrelated aches and pains, but the pain he described seemed too particular to be the result of general ill-health.

'I'm going to bleep Dr Evans,' she told Sarah. 'And this time I'll be at the bedside with him. You go and help the auxiliaries.'

Dr Evans was less than pleased at being called back to the ward. 'I've just examined Mr Benson, Sister, and I don't think there's anything wrong.'

'I'm not happy about that shoulder,' Lisa said calmly. 'If you wouldn't mind examining him again.'

A comment she couldn't quite hear indicated that Dr Evans did mind. He sounded resigned as he said, 'I don't really need this time to study. I'm coming up, Sister.'

Although he was perfectly polite with Mr Benson, it was obvious that he thought this was a wasted journey. He palpated the arm and shoulder, asked when the pain had first started and how the patient felt in general. Outside the little room once more he said, 'Nothing new wrong with him, Sister. All he needs is rest and painkillers, and they've been prescribed already. Now, if there's nothing else...'

'I think we should send for the consultant,' Lisa said flatly.

Dr Evans looked at her, startled. 'Whatever for? I've just told you, there's no need. Sister, doctors diagnose, nurses treat.'

'This is my ward and I'm responsible for it. I want Sir Arthur to look at that shoulder.' Inwardly Lisa was quailing—she knew she was exceeding her authority.

Dr Evans looked at her in disbelief. Then he said, 'By all means, send for him. I know he's in the hospital. Whether he'll be pleased at being disturbed I don't know.'

They were now in Lisa's little office. She phoned the consultant's secretary, who said that Sir Arthur would be along shortly. Lisa and Dr Evans sat waiting in frozen silence.

There was no specialist registrar in Infectious Diseases at the moment, although one had been appointed and would be joining them shortly. This meant that for a while the consultant, Sir Arthur Miles, had to work harder than ever. Lisa hoped he wouldn't think this was a wasted visit.

There was a tap at the door and Sir Arthur entered, a man of medium build, dapper, with highly polished shoes and his signature blue bow tie. Lisa knew that under that unassuming exterior was a brilliant medical mind.

'A little problem?' he asked gently as Lisa offered him the case notes. 'I thought Mr Benson was doing just fine.'

Suddenly Paul Evans went up in Lisa's estimation. Before she could answer he said, 'Sister spotted some-

thing that I'd missed, Sir. It might be nothing but I—
we—thought you ought to see it.'

Keen eyes flashed from sister to doctor. 'I see,' Sir
Arthur said mildly. 'Well, let's take a look.'

His examination didn't seem to be any more de-
tailed than Paul's had been, though Lisa knew he was
seeing far, far more. As ever, Sir Arthur managed to
talk to his patient as he touched and pressed so Mr
Benson seemed quite relaxed. Finally, rather to his
surprise, Paul was asked to take a blood sample and
Lisa to organise an X-ray. Then the three went back
to Lisa's room.

The blood was dispatched to the lab for analysis.
The results would be back in a few hours. Sir Arthur
said, 'Well spotted. We need confirmation, of course,
but I would guess that Mr Benson has reactive arthritis. If there's septicaemia it could be quite serious—but I think we've caught it in time.'

'What treatment will you prescribe, sir?' Paul
asked.

'Oh, at this early stage, none. When the results
come through from the lab we'll make a decision.
Once again, well done.'

Sir Arthur went to the door, smiled his reassuring
smile and said as he left, 'See you tomorrow evening,
Lisa.'

Paul sat silent for a moment. Then he said, 'There's
a lot to learn in medicine. I'll go and look up reactive
arthritis.' Lisa grinned as he left.

The next thing to do was to tell Sarah that she had
been right. Lisa firmly believed it was all-important
to praise her staff when they got things right. After
all, she didn't hesitate to do the opposite when they
got things wrong.

'It was just luck,' Sarah said dismissively. 'Paul would have seen it the next time around. Anyway, I'm glad we can do something for Mr Benson. He's a tough old bird.'

She glanced down at the watch pinned to her apron. 'Soon be time for handover. I'll be round at your flat about three tomorrow, Lisa.'

Lisa looked confused. 'Are you sure you still want to? After all, it's Saturday. Is there nothing else you want to do?'

Sarah shook her head. 'You've spent a lot of time coaching me, and I'd like to do something in return. Besides, I want to keep my hand in—and I've been waiting for the chance to get at you. You need a change.'

Sarah says I need a change, Lisa thought. Perhaps I do.

Lisa lived in her own little custom-built one-bedroomed flat. Until two years ago she had lived with her family—but now they were scattered. She loved them all dearly but she had to admit that she now liked her little bit of independence and self-indulgence. From the corner of her sitting room she could see the sea—just. She enjoyed having a place of her own.

By three o'clock she had finished her washing and all the little household duties that had piled up, and was waiting for Sarah. Tonight was the Blazes Ball— a fund-raising event for her hospital. Tickets were sixty pounds each, and all the senior members of the hospital and local dignitaries would be there.

She was going as Sir Arthur's partner. 'The meal will be excellent,' he had said, 'but the speeches will be boring. I should know, I'm giving one. However, the dancing is quite fun and, if we stick to the waltz, quickstep and foxtrot, I'm sure I won't disgrace you.'

'I'd really love to come,' Lisa had said.

It wasn't the first time he had invited her to formal functions. She knew he found her dependable, and a defence against the wives of the other consultants who felt that he should remarry. And she found him good company—he reminded her a little of her father. If other people found it strange, well, she didn't care. She and Sir Arthur were a good professional team.

But, just for once, she was feeling restive. Life seemed to be passing her by. She felt she'd like to go to the ball with someone—well, nearer her age. She'd had relationships before, but never one that had made her feel that this was the one that counted. And she'd like to. She was now twenty-eight. When she thought of her friends from school she realised that nearly all were married and had had children. A couple had been married, had had children and were now divorced. Now there was a thought!

So, egged on by Sarah, she'd decided that tonight would be—different. She'd bought a midnight blue dress, rather low cut, spending what was for her a ludicrous amount of money. And Sarah was coming round to dress her hair and help her with her make-up.

Her doorbell rang, and from the intercom Sarah's voice called, 'It's me.' Feeling a little apprehensive, Lisa pressed the switch that opened the door.

'I've been itching to get at your hair for months,' Sarah announced. 'It's a glorious red—why don't you do more with it?' With a comb, she lifted a strand from Lisa's forehead and let it fall again.

Lisa was sitting in her bathroom, a towel round her shoulders. 'It's convenient for the job,' she mumbled. 'Nurses don't want hair flying all over the place.' Her hair was short. All it needed was a quick pass with a brush first thing every morning and then she forgot about it.

'If you've got it, flaunt it. I know people who would kill for hair like this. You're going to be the best-looking woman in the room.'

'Well, just for tonight,' Lisa said uneasily.

'Fine. But when I've finished with you I'll bet no one ever forgets you.' Sarah began spraying.

Lisa had never quite realised that some of the skills of a hairdresser were similar to those of a nurse. Sarah kept her at her ease, explained what she was doing and why and showed considerable dexterity.

She was a good teacher, too. As Lisa's hair was drying she showed her how to apply her new make-up. 'Your eyes are a wonderful blue so you must di-rect people's attention to them. Now, look how a line here...' she drew with a dark pencil '...will make the colour seem even bluer.'

Finally it was done. Sarah whisked the towel away, brushed energetically and then led Lisa to the full-length mirror in her bedroom. Lisa blinked. This wasn't Sister Grey!

She knew she was reasonably attractive but, apart from her red hair, had thought herself nothing out of the ordinary. But look at her now!

Her dress was a bit daring, and with her new bra the rich blue sheen of the silk emphasised the swell of her breasts and the creamy skin that redheads often had. Her hair contrasted well, a wild, brilliant halo.

Her eyes shone blue, accentuated by the clever use of mascara.

'I don't look like that. That's not me,' she said, unbelieving.

'Oh, it is you,' Sarah said. 'This is the you that's underneath. I've always known it's been there. You just needed bringing out.'

Sarah stayed for a sherry and then left. Lisa waited for Sir Arthur to call, a vague feeling of excitement and anticipation churning in her stomach. Perhaps tonight would be different.

From her window she saw the old black Rolls Royce pull up outside and Sir Arthur walk to the entrance hall. She knew he liked things to be done properly—he wouldn't want her to be waiting for him downstairs.

When he entered her flat he noticed the change in her appearance at once. 'Goodness, my dear, you look—extravagant tonight,' he said. For him she knew this was praise indeed.

'I feel a bit like Cinderella,' she said. 'Would you like a sherry before we go?'

The ball was being held in the formal rooms of Lacombe Grange, a grand old home built in earlier, more opulent days. Lisa had been there before and had been overawed by the crystal chandeliers, the rich red satin curtains, the white and gold paint on the walls. Tonight, for some reason, she felt happy and at home. She had changed her image—perhaps her life would change. She felt a tiny dart of anticipation.

The reception was being held in the Great Hall. Afterwards they would move into the dining room and then the ballroom. Sir Arthur captured a glass of champagne for each of them, and they chatted. She knew quite a few people there—the hospital chief executive, some of the consultants with their wives. She was particularly pleased to see Mike Gee, the youngish Casualty consultant, and his wife, Liz.

'Lisa, you look absolutely stunning,' Liz said. 'That's a wonderful dress.'

'Stonehouse's sale,' Lisa said, naming a local department store, 'but I did lash out a bit.'

'I'll get down there tomorrow. Mike, don't you think Lisa looks well tonight?'

'I certainly do,' Mike said, 'but I'd rather have her in uniform and in my department.'

Sir Arthur placed an arm round her waist. 'I'm afraid Sister Grey already has a position,' he said. 'Don't poach!'

Laughing, they all walked on. 'You're the belle of the ball,' Sir Arthur said. 'I think I'll ask the chief executive for money for a new nurse for the ward.'

'He's not that smitten,' Lisa said.

The dinner was as good as Sir Arthur had said it would be. Afterwards there were the speeches. Lisa thought they were mercifully short but just a little too gloomy. All that talk about money! Then it was Sir Arthur's turn, and he started, 'I came to a meeting of medical men and found myself listening to a set of bankers.' There was a round of laughter and applause. His was the last speech, and when he had finished the company stood and drifted next door to the ballroom. The business of the evening had not finished, but was just beginning.

Tables surrounded the polished dance floor. As Lisa and Sir Arthur were led to the table reserved for them, she noticed with a hidden grin that it had two extra chairs. No one stayed at their own table.

Sir Arthur ordered a bottle of champagne and then led her onto the floor for an enjoyable dance. When they returned to their table there was a paediatric professor from the local university waiting. 'Just thought I'd pop over for a chat, Arthur,' he said, after the usual introductions and courtesies. 'Now, about the new...' Demurely, Lisa hid her smile.

Mike Gee came over and asked her for a dance. 'Liz is on a couple of hospital committees,' he explained. 'She's seen someone who can help her with some equipment, and she's stalking him.'

'It's like a great bazaar,' Lisa agreed as they swirled around in the centre of the floor. 'Look at them all. And it's not hunters and hunted. They're all hunters.'

'They are, indeed.'

It was an open joke at the hospital that more important decisions were taken on this night than at any hospital committee meeting. All unofficial, of course, but probably more binding because of that.

Mike returned her to her seat and she found Sir Arthur now deep in conversation with John Leckie, the cardiac consultant, and his wife, Alison. 'I must ask you—where did you go to get your hair done?' Alison asked. 'It looks so nice.'

'It was done by Sarah Rogers, one of the nurses on my ward,' Lisa said.

'One of your nurses! John, see if you've got anyone on your ward you can swap for this Nurse Rogers!'

'No deal,' Lisa said, smiling. 'But I'll give her your name if you like.'

John and Alison left—not for their own table, Lisa noticed—and Sir Arthur said, 'If you could just excuse me a moment, Lisa, I—'

'You go,' Lisa said. 'I'll be perfectly all right on my own for a while.'

And she was. More people she knew came over and chatted. She was enjoying herself, among friends. But...there was no magic to the evening. Her new dress, her new image, were fun—but they'd made no difference to her evening. Still, what had she been expecting? Only Cinderella met Prince Charming.

It happened during one of the periods when Sir Arthur had returned to their table, but was deep in conversation with another doctor. Lisa let her gaze wander round the room, looking at new alliances being formed, new proposals being discussed.

At the far end of the room a man entered. In his dark dinner jacket there was nothing at first to distinguish him from all the others there, but for some reason he caught her eye.

He stood confidently, slowly looking round the room. His gaze passed her table—then flashed back. For a moment he appeared to be staring straight at her. She caught her breath in confusion, but refused to look down. Instead, she let her gaze stray to the dancers.

When she glanced upwards he was moving round the floor, threading his way through the maze of tables. She saw him smiling, waiting, apologising. She couldn't keep her eyes off him.

As he got closer she could see him in more detail. His dinner jacket hadn't been cleverly cut to disguise a paunch. He was taller than most of the men who eddied around him, and she noted the easy way he caught a waitress who backed into him. He must be strong.

With hammering heart she suddenly realised that

she was staring, and that he'd caught her doing so. He smiled at her, and after a tentative return smile she wrenched her gaze away. She raised her glass. It was easier to pretend to drink, while looking at him covertly.

He wasn't what she'd call a really good-looking man. His dark hair was too short. He looked almost a bruiser, with high cheek-bones, the skin and muscles of his face taut. But when he smiled, as he was doing now...

'Sir Arthur, I'm a gatecrasher. But you said to come if I could.' It was a warm voice, with just a touch of West Country burr. Lisa's mother had been an actress, and had taught her daughter always to listen to voices. This voice was warm and comforting, transforming his rather bleak face—just as his smile did. It made him approachable. Just for a moment Lisa wondered if he knew this was the effect he made—and traded on it.

'Alex, my dear chap, how good to see you!' Sir Arthur didn't need to say how pleased he was—it was obvious. 'Let me introduce you. Lisa, this is Alex Scott, my new specialist registrar. Alex, this is Lisa Grey, the best ward sister in the hospital. She was away on a course when you looked round last month. And, as unpaid extra duty, she accompanies me to functions where I'm likely to be harassed if I'm on my own. I don't know what I'd do without her.'

Now Alex looked at Lisa directly—his eyes were as blue as hers. But were they guileless? Eyes, she believed, were the windows of the soul. She'd spent most of her nursing career in a casualty department, and she'd got used to looking into people's eyes. So many people there, from road accidents or domestic incidents, had something to hide. She wondered if she was wrong to detect wariness in this man's eyes.

'Sister, it's good to meet you,' he was saying. 'Sir Arthur told me that working with you was one of the benefits of this job.'

'All Sir Arthur wants is his own way,' she said with a smile. 'I hope you like working hard.'

His hand clasp was firm, without being forceful. She thought he held her hand just a little longer than was really necessary.

Sir Arthur, meanwhile, was vigorously waving at a waiter to fetch another glass. 'I'm really glad you've come, Alex,' he said. 'There are a couple of things we need to sort out. I...'

Lisa wanted to stay, she really did. But she knew Sir Arthur of old. If there were things he wanted to discuss with Alex he'd do it best on his own. Rising, she said, 'This is a good time for me to go and have a word about the hospital friends' committee. Will you excuse me?'

Sir Arthur and Alex both came to their feet. 'Of course,' Sir Arthur said urbanely. Alex said, 'You are coming back?' He seemed quite anxious.

'I'll be back,' she assured him. His obvious wish to see her again quite excited her.

There were one or two ladies she had to speak to about the committee, but her business was soon done and so she walked to the ornate cloakroom. She sat in a gold chair in front of a large mirror, carefully repairing the wonderful job Sarah had done on her. It was quite warm, but that didn't explain the sparkle to her eyes, the faint touch of pink in her cheeks, even the warmer tone to her skin. She'd known the man for less than five minutes, but Dr Alex Scott was the most exciting man she'd met in years.

Knowing Sir Arthur, she wasn't entirely surprised to see Alex on his own when she returned to their table. She walked up behind him, admiring his broad shoulders, the column of his neck. She said, 'Hello again.' He came easily to his feet and drew back her chair, settling her carefully.

'Sir Arthur leaves his apologies,' he said, the humour underlying his words quite clear. 'He asked if I'd look after you—or if you'd look after me. I'm glad you're back. I was feeling quite lost. Lonely even.'

She eyed him, perfectly relaxed with a half-smile on his lips. 'You don't look very lonely,' she said drily.

He waved at the scene around him. 'I've got no other friends to run to. I've never seen such a party for wandering from table to table. It's like one of those children's games. I expect the music to stop, and everyone will have to pretend to be statues.'

She giggled. 'Networking,' she explained. 'Don't let the smiles fool you. This is the only occasion when all the money men and all the senior clinical staff are together. There are a lot of decisions being taken out there.'

He grimaced. 'I know. These days all hospitals are the same. Still, if in the end— Ah!'

A waiter bent over the table, showing Alex the label of a bottle. Alex glanced at it and nodded. 'That'll do very well, thank you.'

As the man deftly pulled the cork with a satisfying pop, Alex explained, 'I took the liberty of ordering another bottle. I hope you'll join me?'

Normally Lisa drank very little, but she was warm

and she was enjoying herself. Why not? There were only the two of them at the table. Deep inside her she realised she was doing more than enjoy herself. This might—this could—turn into the magic kind of evening she'd been wanting. She knew he was attracted to her. And...

She'd only just met him. Forcing herself to be calm, she asked, 'You'll be coming onto the ward next week?'

'I certainly hope to. There are a few bits of local organising to do, but I'm looking forward to starting work.'

'Where are you from? Certainly not around here.'

Laughing, he shook his head. 'I've been near Bristol for the past four years and I needed a change, but I wanted to be near another seaport. I also wanted to work with Sir Arthur. You know he has the reputation of being a bit of an alarmist in the medical press? About the spread of bacteria that are resistant to antibiotics?'

'You mean his article on methycillin-resistant staphylococcus aureus?' Lisa asked calmly. 'Yes, I read it.'

'You know about MRSA?'

'Nurses can read as well as doctors.'

He laughed again. 'Sorry, sorry! Well, I think Sir Arthur is right, and I wanted to work with him. So, when the job was advertised, I applied.'

He sipped his champagne. 'It's always interesting, coming to a new job. You make new friends, even hear new accents.' He smiled at her, quickly, even intimately, and her heart bounded. 'You're also not from around here, are you?'

'No,' she said, both pleased and surprised. 'Can you tell that from my accent?'

'I think so. Is there a tiny touch of Welsh there?'

'Not bad. I'm from Shropshire, actually. Quite near the Welsh border.' She mentioned the little town where she'd been born, where she'd spent the first twenty-six years of her life.

'I've been through it,' he said. 'Why move to this great city from that beautiful place?'

There were reasons, but for the moment she didn't want to go into them. After all, she didn't know the man very well. Shrugging, she said, 'Like you, I needed a change. And I was in a rut. And my family...'

It nearly slipped out, and he spotted her hesitation. 'Tell me,' he urged gently.

He was very easy to talk to. She felt at home with him, but they'd only just met and she must keep something back.

The music struck up again and people trooped onto the floor. 'I'm monopolising you,' he said, 'Very happily, I may add, but did you ought to be seeing other people? Networking yourself?'

She giggled. 'No, you're not monopolising me and, no, I didn't ought to be seeing other people. I like talking to you.'

'Well, would you like to dance?'

'I'd really love to.'

She'd danced four times already. Sir Arthur, especially, was a very good dancer, but this was different. Alex's arm slid tightly round her and she was aware of his body, of the muscles under the formal suit. His hand held hers gently but there was an electric bonding between them. He was a good dancer and she swayed and moved with him, for a while in a little dream of her own. He didn't speak. When the music stopped she stood still for a moment, not wanting to leave the fragile world she'd created for herself.

But it had to end. Gently he propelled her back to their table. 'You were telling me about your family,' he prompted, and refilled her glass.

Well, she could tell him something. Most of it, in fact. 'My mother was an actress. She...died in a car crash when I was seven. I've got two younger sisters, Emily and Rosalind. We'd always been a close family, and when my mother...died we became closer.'

'With you acting as mother?'

This was too perceptive. 'No, no,' she said hurriedly. 'I loved them as sisters. I love them still.'

'But you were still mother. You couldn't help it.'

'Perhaps, just a bit.' She decided to hurry on to other things. 'Anyway, I trained locally as a nurse, and lived at home while I was training. My sister, Emily, trained as a midwife. She had a bit of a hard time and now she's working in Africa. My youngest sister, Rosalind, is at university here, training to be a doctor. I see her quite often.'

'Three sisters all in the caring professions. None of you wanted to follow your mother? Be an actress?'

'None of us,' she said flatly.

'And your father?'

Her face lit up as she thought of him. How could a man have made such a good job of bringing up three daughters without help? 'He's gone walkabout!' she said. 'Two and a half years ago he said he loved us all, but we had our lives to get on with. We had to separate, get out into the world. And all his life he'd wanted to visit South America. So he was going, leaving us. When he came back we'd be closer than ever.'

'He sounds a very shrewd man,' Alex said, 'and a very loving one. He'd be a hard act to follow. Are you looking for a man like your father?'

She was surprised at this, but not annoyed. It seemed a fair question. 'Perhaps,' she said, 'but I haven't found one yet. Emily was married briefly. When her husband died the pain was almost unbearable—not just for her but for all of us.'

He moved his hand over hers and squeezed it briefly. 'Things pass,' he said. 'You learn to live with the pain.'

'I hope you've not been missing me,' a voice broke in. 'Sorry to leave you so much, Lisa.'

She smiled up at Sir Arthur. 'No, you're not,' she said. 'You enjoy going to other people's tables because you can walk away when you've finished your business.'

He winced. 'There are times when you're too acute, Lisa. Of course, you're quite right. Now, it's half past eleven and I'm on call tomorrow. Please don't let me hurry you but...'

Lisa grinned. This happened every time they went out. Sir Arthur was famous for always wanting to get home at what he called 'a reasonable hour'. She couldn't keep him longer than midnight, but...

Alex looked at her and a message flashed between them, unspoken but as clear as the air in winter. 'Would it be all right if I drove Lisa home?' he asked.

'Well...Lisa?' Sir Arthur looked properly concerned.

'I would like to stay just a little longer, if it's no trouble and Alex doesn't mind driving me back.'

Alex said that it was no trouble and he'd love to drive her back. Sir Arthur said he had enjoyed himself tremendously, then set off for the exit.

'Just watch him,' Lisa said affectionately. 'It'll take him half an hour to get to the door.'

Alex leaned over and touched her arm, a touch that burned like fire. 'He's very lucky to have someone like you as Ward Sister,' he said softly. 'And I'm sure he knows it.'

For a moment the two of them were silent. The noise in the room around them faded and they were aware only of each other.

'Hi, I gather you're the new special reg in Infectious Diseases. I'm Mike Gee, Casualty.'

Lisa looked up, startled. A smiling Mike and Liz were standing at their table. How had they got so close without her noticing? Collecting her wandering thoughts, she made introductions and asked Mike and Liz to sit down. Soon the two men were deep in medical gossip, leaving Liz and Lisa to amuse themselves as best they could.

'I suppose it could be worse,' Liz said resignedly. 'They could be talking about football.'

After ten minutes, however, Liz had had enough. She leaned forward and said, 'This is a dance, not a medical convention. Mike, we're dancing!'

'Yes, dear,' he said, mock-submissively, and rose to his feet.

'Why don't we do the same?' Alex asked, holding out his arms to Lisa.

'Try and stop me,' she said.

By this time the normally staid medical staff were letting themselves go a little. The dancing was noisy, vigorous. Alex picked Lisa up, whirling her round effortlessly, and she marvelled at his strength. When they returned to their table there were more people waiting and she had more introductions to make. Blazes' staff were friendly. It was all very pleasant but she wanted him more to herself.

'I'll never remember all these people,' he whispered to her as they snatched a dance in between conversations. 'I'm getting bewildered. Isn't there anywhere we can go where we can talk in private?' He looked at her cautiously. 'That is, if you want to, of course.'

'It is getting a bit overwhelming,' she agreed. 'I think there's the Garden Room at the back.'

Leaving Lisa at their table, Alex went to explore. She was alone for a moment—and discovered that she was happier than she'd been for years. She felt alive, as if she'd woken from a half-sleep. Then she told herself not to be so foolish. He was just an agreeable man she was going to work with.

He reappeared and once again she felt that odd bumping movement in her chest. 'I've ordered a table in the Garden Room,' he said. 'We can have supper there. A lot of people are leaving now. We can do the same.'

She waved to Mike and Liz, and Alex escorted her to the foyer. 'I must be getting old,' he said. 'I used to love all this noise late at night.'

'You don't look tired,' she said.

He squeezed her arm. 'I don't feel it.'

The Garden Room was smaller, more intimate. At one end there were great windows, opening onto softly illuminated formal gardens. The room was dimly lit, each table with its own tiny lamp.

Quite a few couples were still having supper. Then,

as they were led to their table, a flame suddenly leaped from a table where a waiter was leaning over a silver chafing dish—a great blue flame, about four feet high. She could feel the heat, smell scorching meat.

Lisa couldn't help it. A terrified moan burst from her lips and only Alex's arm, quickly thrown round her waist, stopped her from slumping to the floor.

The waiter was alarmed. 'Is Madam feeling well? I hope the flame didn't surprise you—our flambé dishes are a speciality of the house.'

Somehow she managed to push herself erect, but she still needed Alex's arm round her waist. 'I'm fine,' she said through gritted teeth. 'It was just a shock. Is this our table?'

It was Alex who pulled out the chair and eased her into it. 'We'd like two brandies,' he said quietly. 'My friend just needs to get her breath back.'

He sat by her side. Her body was stiff as she grasped his hand, unable to speak. When the brandy came he spoke to her gently, reassuringly, holding the glass to her lips. She sipped, and as the warmth of the liquid trickled through her she slowly relaxed.

'I'm sorry,' she mumbled. 'Silly of me. It's just that I wasn't expecting it and it came as a bit of a shock.' She knew the explanation sounded lame. Feverishly she continued, 'Now I remember this place is famous for its flambé dishes, they heat alcohol and—'

'Lisa!' His voice was quiet, reassuring. 'Stop talking and drink your brandy. It doesn't matter. Everyone gets a shock at some time.' His hand released hers and his fingertips slid to her wrist. 'Let's play doctors and nurses. Your pulse is fast—but it's slowing.'

'I think I'm all right now.'

She sat in silence as he talked in low tones to the waiter. Their bottle of champagne was fetched from the ballroom, and Alex ordered a light supper. She tasted the brandy again, and her jangling heart slowed down.

'This is a nice room,' she said brightly. 'I've never been here before.' She hoped the events of the past five minutes had been forgotten. They hadn't.

He said, 'It's not my business, if you don't want to tell me, but your reaction was far more than simple shock. It might help to talk about it.'

For quite a while Lisa didn't answer, but he didn't press her. His hand stroked her forearm. It was pleasant, comforting. Finally she spoke.

'It's got to be inside a room. Not in a fireplace, but in a room. Outside is fine, I love barbecues and I love bonfires. But flames inside a room terrify me.'

'I should think they terrify a lot of people,' he said gently. 'Do you know why?'

She shrugged. 'I was always a bit frightened. Perhaps because of something that happened as a child. But then, about three years ago, I was working as a staff nurse in Casualty. There was an old lady who lived just down the road from us. It was the usual story—she lived on her own, damp old cottage, refused to move. The district nurse and Social Services were trying to sort things out, and I got into the habit of dropping in, too. I used to put her to bed at night.'

Memories of that night were crowding back on her, and she could feel her pulse accelerating. But perhaps talking about it to this calm man might lay the devils that sometimes tormented her.

'Anyway, one night I was delayed. These things

happen in Casualty. I was three-quarters of an hour late. The old lady had put herself to bed, but she'd dragged one of those evil paraffin heaters into her bedroom. And it had fallen over. I got in just as her quilt and curtains caught fire. I could see her looking at me, with flames all round her. Well...' Lisa's voice shook as she relived that appalling moment... 'I dragged the quilt off her and pulled her out of bed. Fortunately, she'd just had a telephone installed so I rang the fire brigade and the ambulance. We were both taken back to my own casualty department.' She could tell that her voice was unnaturally high but there was nothing she could do about it.

'You've no idea what it does to your perception of a job to be a patient instead of a nurse. Perhaps it was good for me. Anyway, the old lady was fine. In the ambulance she asked if we could have the siren going.'

'What about you? Were you hurt?'

'A few days in bed. My hands and arms were burned, but not badly enough to need skin grafts. Otherwise a happy ending. The old lady decided to move into sheltered accommodation and she's still there, perfectly content.'

For a while there was silence, and then Alex said, 'The story's not ended. Tell me more.'

He was shrewd—he'd be a good diagnostician. He knew when to listen, when to push.

Sighing, she went on, 'The hospital was quite close to a foundry and we constantly had minor burns coming into Casualty. I found that I just couldn't take it. Any other injury, yes, but not burns. So I decided I needed a change.'

She tried to put on a light-hearted tone. 'I wanted

something as far as possible from the speed of Casualty, something where I could build up a relationship with patients. I thought about Geriatrics, but I finished up in Infectious Diseases.'

Lisa was getting back to normal. Telling her story had somehow eased the tension—he was a good listener and she could now relax. She finished the last drop of her brandy and Alex poured her more champagne. At that moment the waiter reappeared with their supper, a plate covered with titbits, some warm, some cold. It had been quite a while since dinner, she realised, and such a lot had happened to her since then.

They sat and ate and talked. He encouraged her to tell him about her family, and they were nearly the last in the Garden Room when he said that perhaps they ought to go. Outside, the car park was nearly deserted.

'I hope this thing starts,' he said, unlocking a medium-sized nondescript car. 'I'm not very happy with it. It's a courtesy car. I've just ordered a new one to celebrate my new job.'

But it started first time. Lisa decided that it was that kind of night. 'I have enjoyed the evening, and your company, Alex,' she said, and impulsively leaned forward and kissed him. 'And I'm very much looking forward to working with you.'

Kissing someone like that wasn't something she normally did. In fact, she'd never done it before. But tonight, she decided, was different.

He turned, reached for her. His kiss was gentle at first, but then she felt the urgency growing in him and knew she was going to respond. Her arms wrapped round him, pulled him closer.

After a minute he gently disengaged himself. 'Where do you live, Lisa?' he asked.

She was a little disappointed, but after all, a hotel car park was still a bit public. She directed him to her block of flats. As they drove she chattered happily about Blazes Hospital, about the staff, the happy atmosphere. When he could he held her hand, and in no time they were outside her home.

Should she invite him in for coffee? Ordinarily Lisa wouldn't have dreamed of it, but she and Alex seemed to get on so well. They'd only met this evening and she felt she'd known him for ever. 'Would you like to—' she started.

Laying his hand on her arm, he interrupted her, his voice gentle, even apologetic.

'Lisa, there's something I should have said before. I'm sorry, and I hope it doesn't make any difference to us. I've got a family, a boy and a girl. Holly is seven, she's not sleeping well and I—'

'Can't her mother look after her?' Lisa's evening was ruined, her meaningless question echoing between them.

'No, she can't,' he said heavily. 'She's in America. But—'

'I'm looking forward to meeting her and your family.' Lisa knew her voice was too bright, too shrill. 'Now, don't get out, I'm home. I'll see you next week on the ward.' Then she was out of the car and running across the car park.

Somehow she opened the doors, ran upstairs and stared through the darkened curtains. His car was still there. After five minutes it pulled away. Only then did she burst into tears.

CHAPTER TWO

SUNDAY wasn't good.

In spite of her late night, Lisa was up early, tearing round the flat—washing, tidying, cleaning. When there was positively nothing else to clean there were letters to write to her father and sister, Emily. In each she mentioned that she'd been to the Blazes Ball with Sir Arthur, and had met the new specialist registrar, who seemed pleasant and quite competent.

Then there was her reading. She believed that nurses should keep up to date with the latest developments, and carefully read articles in the *Nursing Times* and the *Journal of Infectious Diseases*. She made a few notes.

She got through the morning without thinking— well, without thinking very much. Since she was a child she'd known that the worst thing to do with a problem was to brood on it. The best thing to do was work.

Someone rang her bell at about twelve. Thinking it might be her sister, Rosalind, Lisa opened the door, a welcoming smile on her face. The smile died when she saw her caller. It was Alex Scott, a bunch of yellow roses casually hanging from his hand and a most determined expression on his face.

She was stricken. He was the last person she wanted to call. Feebly she tried to close the door. He pressed it back open and stepped forward so she was forced to back into her little hall. He seemed awfully large.

It only took seconds for her to recover her poise. The anger she had felt the night before flooded through her afresh.

'This isn't a good time for casual callers,' she snarled. 'And shouldn't you spend your weekends with your wife and family?'

He winced at her venom. Carefully he laid the flowers on her hall table. 'I brought these as a small peace offering,' he said, 'but I doubt they'll work. Just let me tell you one fact and then I'll go. I am not married, I have no wife.'

'But your children…?'

'I was married. I am now divorced.'

The silence between them seemed to stretch into infinity. 'You do believe me?' he asked eventually.

Lisa thought for a moment. 'Yes, I believe you. I suppose you'd better come in. And thank you for the flowers. It wasn't necessary.'

'I think it was,' he said.

Finding a vase and filling it with water gave her something to do, something to occupy her hands while chaotic thoughts stormed in her mind. She decided not to offer him a drink—she just couldn't cope with him sitting comfortably in her living room. Finally she had to face him, looking at that brooding face that had so thrilled her the night before. That still thrilled her, in fact.

'I can't stay long,' Alex said. 'Holly is missing me—she gets a bit clinging at times. But I think I owe you an explanation. I was married and I have two children. My wife was a doctor—a very ambitious one. She was given the chance to train in

America four years ago. The children haven't seen her since. Six months ago she phoned to say that she'd met a man in Boston and that the marriage was over. The divorce is now through.'

Lisa just couldn't deal with this. She didn't know how to feel. Had her anger, her misery of the night before, been in vain? She took refuge in meaningless politeness, forgetting her previous decision. 'Would you like some tea?'

'I think I would,' he said.

It gave her another respite, hurrying round for mugs and the kettle, but soon she had to face him again.

'I wanted to get things straight between us,' he said. 'I do feel that to a certain extent I was unfair to you. I should have told you about my family earlier in the evening. It was just that I was enjoying your company and I didn't want to complicate things.'

'So you conveniently hid them.' She could feel the anger growing in her again, but this time she knew that it wasn't entirely justified. She would have to explain to him.

'You probably thought that my reaction last night was a bit excessive,' she said. 'Well, there is a reason. You know I told you my mother was killed in a car crash when I was seven?'

He nodded, his eyes alert.

'Perhaps because of that I've always felt envious of families who had a mother.'

'It's a very natural reaction,' he said softly.

'Natural! That's one word for it.' She took a breath. Her heart was beating faster. Even now, after twenty-odd years, when she thought of it there was still the acid taste of betrayal.

'My mother left her husband and three daughters

to go and live with another man. She said family life was stifling her. The man was an old producer friend. He'd been visiting her for weeks—taking her to plays, introducing her to old friends, telling her she had a career in front of her. He deliberately set out to...to make her unhappy. Afterwards we found out he'd done it before to another married woman. It was just casual pleasure to him.'

She tried to control her shaking voice. The next bit was the worst. The sheer unfairness of it still shocked her.

'But she never knew. Three weeks after she left us they were both killed in a car crash. He was drunk.'

Alex reached out to touch her tentatively on the shoulder, a gesture of comfort. She shook off his hand.

'Since then I've hated anyone who breaks up a marriage, especially one where there are children. And most...most of all I hate people who treat sex as a game. Sex without love is nothing.'

'I agree with you,' he said, 'well, up to a point.'

In the afternoon Sir Arthur phoned, as courteous as ever. He wanted to know if Lisa had got home safely and if she'd enjoyed being with Alex. 'He seems a very clever man,' he said. 'The hospital is lucky to have him.'

'I'm very much looking forward to working with him,' Lisa said evenly. 'When will he start?'

There was a chuckle at the other end of the line. 'Earlier than he anticipated. I'm needed rather urgently in London. I've just phoned him—Dr Scott starts tomorrow. Look after him for me, Lisa.' Sir Arthur rang off.

Tomorrow! Lisa had been expecting a couple of days' grace, some time to get used to the idea of having the man on her ward. But he was starting tomorrow.

Usually Lisa quite liked going back to work on Monday morning. This time she was just a little apprehensive. She'd have to work with Alex Scott. How would they get on together—professionally, that is?

She had to admit that the department needed a new specialist registrar. They'd been without one for six weeks now, and the strain was telling on Sir Arthur. Alex could only make things easier—for him at least.

First there was handover. With Ann Pytchley, the night Sister, she skimmed over the patients' notes. There had been no new admissions. Blood tests had confirmed that Sir Arthur's diagnosis of reactive arthritis in Mr Benson's shoulder had been correct. He'd come in on Saturday morning and prescribed treatment.

After giving her staff their initial tasks, Lisa walked round the ward. She said hello to all her patients, gently chided a couple of them who had been awkward about taking their medication and listened to the odd complaint. Most patients in Infectious Diseases tended to be older, and Lisa knew they valued a personal visit from the sister.

Sarah had been on earlies, starting her shift two hours before Lisa arrived. They only had time for a quick smile when they first met, but later in the morning, as Lisa was sitting down to a vast quantity of paperwork, Sarah slipped in for a coffee and a quick chat.

'Come on, tell me all about it,' she said. 'Did you have a good time?'

'Super,' said Lisa, falsely bright. 'I really enjoyed myself. And a lot of people asked about your hairdo.'

Sarah was sensitive, realising that Lisa was keeping something back. 'I didn't do it as part of an advertising campaign,' she said bluntly. 'What went wrong?'

'Nothing at all went wrong. Just the same as before—the same old faces. Oh, and I met the new specialist registrar. Name's Alex Scott. He'll be in later.'

'Do you like him?' Sarah probed.

'I'm sure he'll be a good doctor. He's got a couple of kids.'

'I see,' said Sarah, and Lisa wondered what, if anything, she'd let slip.

Trouble started an hour later with a call from Casualty. 'Got one for you,' the senior house officer in Infectious Diseases said. 'Marie Pinckney, age mid-twenties going on fifty. Found collapsed in the street. I've sent blood off for testing, but from her jaundiced colour I'd make an informed guess that she's got hepatitis.'

'An addict?' Lisa asked.

'You can see the needle tracks on her arms. I had difficulty finding a vein to put a line into. They'd all shut down.'

Lisa sighed. 'Send her up. I'll get a bed ready.'

It was a hospital's job to treat anybody, a nurse's job to tend anybody. Moral judgements didn't come into it, but when Lisa saw the mess people made of their own lives she felt sorry.

Mainlining addicts tended to share needles. Clean needles were available free at the drug centre in town but often addicts just didn't bother. So if any of them were infected then diseases like septicaemia or infective hepatitis were easily passed along. Lisa had even seen a case of malaria caught through a dirty needle.

She phoned Sir Arthur's secretary and asked her to send up Alex Scott when it was convenient. Then she collected Paul Evans and went to prepare a bed for their new admission.

It was impossible not to feel sorry for Marie when she arrived. Her skin and eyes were an unhealthy yellow, her hair straggled and her teeth badly needed attention. And she was malnourished. The outlines of bones showed through the greasy skin. 'Sorry to be a trouble, Nurse,' she murmured.

Gently Lisa squeezed her hand. 'You're no trouble,' she lied. 'We'll soon get you well again.'

With Lisa in attendance, Paul carefully examined the wrecked body. Pulse, blood pressure, heart, reflexes—all were carefully checked. Then there was nothing he could do until the results of the blood test came back. 'I'll be back later, Sister,' he said, and left.

Lisa decided to give Marie a blanket bath—she certainly needed one. As she did so she chatted, trying to make the girl feel at ease. With a shock she realised that her patient wasn't far off her own age.

For a while Marie lay limp, her eyes closed. But after a while her eyes opened and she made some attempt to ease Lisa's task. Lisa thought she could see gratitude in her eyes. She wondered how much tenderness and concern there had been in Marie's life.

'Marie, have you any family we can get in touch with?' she asked gently.

Marie shook her head. 'They chucked me out. Well, I suppose I left, really. But they don't want to see me.' After a long pause she went on, 'I've got this feller, he'll be in to see me. Perhaps. He's been good to me.'

'He's been good to you. Is he a…?'

'Is he a junkie, like me? Oh, yes. We have to stick together, you know.'

'There is help available,' Lisa ventured.

'Help?' The laugh turned into a spasm of coughing. 'People despise us. Even that doctor does. He tried to hide it, but I could see it in his eyes.'

'No one despises anyone in hospital,' Lisa said. 'We're here to help people. Have you ever been on a programme?'

'To get me off drugs? Yes, I've been on a programme but they never work. You try for a day or two…then you slide back.'

Lisa was aware that Marie was getting restless. 'This doctor that's coming to see me,' she said anxiously. 'He will give me something, won't he? I mean, I just can't manage without. He will give me something, won't he?'

'I'm sure you'll be all right,' Lisa soothed. 'There's methadone. And no more dirty needles!'

Marie tried to smile. 'I think I'll sleep a while,' she said. 'And thanks for the bath. I feel so much better.'

Paul was busy writing up his notes when Lisa entered her office. 'Sad case,' he said. 'We get them better—if we can. Then they go and ruin all our good work.'

'I know,' Lisa said. She thought for a minute. It wasn't her place to interfere with the doctors—the nurses were her responsibility. Still, she liked young Paul. Bracing herself, she said, 'Marie said she thought you despised her. She could tell by the way you looked at her.'

He froze. She could see the tension in his body, the tendons in his neck standing out. Then he sighed, and made an obvious attempt to relax. In a resigned tone he said, 'That's not the message we want to get across, is it, Sister? I'll watch it in future. This medicine is a lot harder than I thought when I started seven years ago.'

Lisa gave a wry grin. Paul Evans would make a good doctor in time.

She was alone in her office when Alex tapped and came in. For a moment the two of them looked at each other, and Lisa was transported back to a happier time. He was wonderful. She knew she would never forget the night at the Blazes Ball.

'Lisa…' he said hesitantly.

She interrupted him. 'Sorry to call you so soon, Doctor, but we have a new admission, a young drug addict, and I think you should see her as quickly as possible.'

'Of course. But, Lisa—'

'I don't want to keep her waiting any longer than necessary.'

He got the message. They were professionals together—but that was all for the moment. 'Very well,' he said. 'If I could have a quick look at her case notes.'

She handed him the notes Paul had just finished, and as he read through them she studied him surreptitiously.

He was dressed in the usual white coat, but with formal dark trousers, a crisp white shirt and college tie. She approved. Many of their patients were older, and they liked a doctor to look like a doctor. Informality here wasn't a good idea, as it might have been in Paediatrics or Casualty.

She couldn't help looking at him. She felt the rush of emotions she'd experienced on Saturday night. There was anticipation, excitement, the thrill of being next to a man who was obviously attracted to her. Still, right now she was a nurse.

Paul came into the office. He'd met Alex before. There was a quick exchange of greetings and then the three of them went to Marie's room. Lisa was impressed with Alex's bedside manner.

'Hello, Marie, what's been happening to you?' he asked courteously. Then there was quite a lengthy conversation before he started any kind of examination. Lisa realised that not only had Alex put Marie at her ease but he'd also learned quite a lot. She also noticed that Alex took pains to bring Paul into the conversation. He was a good medical teacher.

Halfway through the examination there came the sound of raised voices outside. Alex frowned. Lisa excused herself and left.

Outside she found Sarah, arguing with an unpleasant-looking young man in dirty trainers, tracksuit bottoms and an old anorak. As she got closer she could see he had a pale unshaven face. From the man's attitude she guessed he was high on something. Closer still, she discovered he smelled of alcohol.

'Who're you, then?' the man asked offensively.

She could cope with people like this. 'I am Sister Grey, and this is my ward, Mr…?'

'You've got my woman here and I want to see her.'

'Your woman?' Lisa asked with distaste. 'Do you

mean Miss Pinckney? If you'd like to come into my office we can talk about her.'

'I don't want to come in your office! I want to see Marie!' Now he was shouting.

'Listen,' Lisa snapped, 'this is my ward and you're disturbing my patients. If you want to talk to me get in that office now.' She pulled out a bleeper. 'Otherwise I'll call Hospital Security and in ten minutes you'll be in a police cell.'

The man hesitated. 'Don't think I don't mean it,' Lisa advised. 'D'you want to spend the night in the cells?' She stepped closer, staring into his watery eyes.

She'd beaten him. His eyes flickered and looked away. 'I just want to see that she's all right,' he mumbled.

'That's what we all want. Now, sit in my office over there and I'll come to see you in a moment.' He did as he was told.

'I hope I never get on the wrong side of you, Sister,' Sarah muttered. 'You scared him and you scared me, too.'

'Just play-acting,' Lisa said.

She didn't get much out of Brian Barnes. He confirmed the address that Marie had managed to give, said they lived together and that she had no other family but him.

'You realise how ill she is?' Lisa asked. 'We're still making tests, but we think she has hepatitis B. At the moment her illness is serious, but not dangerous. The situation could get worse.'

'You mean she could die?' There seemed to be genuine concern in his shifty eyes.

'Not if she looks after herself. We'll keep her here

for a while—see to her diet, treat her condition as best we can. Definitely no alcohol or any stimulants like that.' When he said nothing she went on, 'She'll have to go on a programme, you know. Drugs and this disease just don't mix.'

'That's what you think,' came the sullen retort. 'Never mind the drugs—just get her better.'

Alex entered, and she had to admit that she was pleased to see him. She introduced Barnes to him, and said he had come to see Marie.

Alex didn't offer to shake hands. 'You were making that noise outside?' he asked abruptly.

'Didn't know where she was.'

'In future kindly remember this is a hospital.'

She hadn't entirely realised how intimidating Alex could be when he didn't smile. The muscular body was bad enough, but the glacial look he gave Barnes seemed enough to shrivel him.

'I'll take you to see her now. You may speak to her but you are not to touch her. Is that clear?'

'I'll take Mr Barnes, Doctor,' Lisa said. 'It is my job.'

'Thank you, Sister. This once I'll do your job.'

She wasn't sorry. Dealing with people like Brian Barnes was always a strain. She decided to get on with her paperwork.

Five minutes later Alex re-entered her room. 'Nasty piece of work,' he said. 'I've put him in the lift and phoned Security to make sure he leaves the premises.'

'Good idea,' she said shortly.

'I've got a couple of students, doing the round with me in half an hour,' he said. 'I'll see you then.'

She had to work with this man, establish some kind of professional relationship with him. He seemed to be a good doctor, it was just a pity that—'I'm going to have a cup of coffee now,' she said. 'Would you like to wait here and have one?'

'I'd like that very much. I don't think there's much we can do yet for Marie. Bed rest and symptom relief for a week or so. Certainly we can't use interferon yet.'

'I hope the treatment works,' Lisa said, busying herself with the kettle.

'It will—if she can keep off the drugs. And I know that's a big if. She was once quite an attractive girl.'

It wasn't just a detached observation, Lisa realised. He felt genuine pity for Marie. He hadn't built that outer hardness that too many doctors acquired.

'Incidentally, I heard you dealing with Barnes. I was going to come out but I thought you did a good job. You can fight when you want to, can't you, Sister?'

'I can fight,' she said. 'Especially when I'm threatened.'

'I know you can. But addicts can be unpredictable. I've a feeling we're going to have trouble with Barnes.'

'Don't tell me. The one thing an addict hates is a fellow addict trying to break the habit.'

They sat, sipping coffee. Then Alex said abruptly, 'Lisa, there are things that have to be sorted out between us. Saturday night happened. We can't just forget it.'

'Just a pleasant evening. It was good of you to take me to the Garden Room.'

'Just a pleasant evening? I enjoyed myself more than I have done in months. And I thought you felt the same way. That red hair of yours was glorious. What happened to it, by the way?'

It was nearly back to her old style—neat, close to her head. 'I changed it. You can't have a sister on a ward with hair frizzing all over the place.'

'It didn't frizz all over the place. It made you look like some wild Welsh goddess.'

She bowed her head over her coffee, not wanting him to see how much she appreciated the compliment. 'What did you want to say about Saturday night?'

'I was wrong not to tell you I had been married, that I had children. I'd just met you and I'd never met someone as attractive as you, someone who was so much fun just to be with. I was enjoying your company so much.'

'I enjoyed your company, too,' she said quietly.

'So why can't we start again? We work together, we can be friends—why can't we have something else? A relationship free of commitment on both sides.'

'Free of commitment? Dr Scott, to me a relationship means commitment.'

He frowned. 'Lisa, I've just been through one very messy marriage. I have my children to think of. There is no way I'll risk their happiness—and mine—by making the same mistake again. I just don't want to get involved with anyone.'

'And I won't have any relationship without commitment and involvement.'

He looked at her bleakly. 'Then I guess the conversation is closed.'

It was raining as Lisa left the hospital that evening. She drove her Fiesta out of the staff car park—and there was Alex Scott, looking disbelievingly into his car boot.

Her first reaction was to drive past and splash him. But she didn't. Instead, she pulled up alongside. 'Trouble?' she asked sweetly.

He looked at her broodingly, rain dripping from his hair down his face. 'Some courtesy car. I've got a puncture in the front tyre and the spare is flat, too.'

She looked at the name of the garage on the side of the car. 'I can either take you to the garage or drop you off at home. Where d'you live?'

'Not too far from you. And I think I'd prefer to go home.' He named a street she recognised as being quite close to her flat. Somehow its nearness made her wary.

'It's good of you to pick me up,' he said as she negotiated the evening traffic. 'I wouldn't have been surprised if you'd driven by.'

'Don't think I didn't consider it. And there was a puddle just by the side of your car.'

'You're a frightening woman, Sister Grey,' he growled.

'I just fight back when I think it's needed.'

It was still raining when she pulled up outside the house he said he was renting, an old-fashioned Victorian building surrounded by shrubbery. 'I don't want to hide anything more from you,' he said. 'Would you like to come in and meet the family?'

Her first reaction was to say no. Then, like an itch that had to be scratched, she knew she'd say yes. She wanted to know as much about him as she could—even if it did hurt.

'I'd like to,' she said, 'but before we go inside tell me their names, then I'll know who I'm meeting.'

'You're shrewd,' he said. 'I can see why you're such a valued sister. My mother lives with us—she's Lucy. Then I have two kids—a girl, Holly, aged seven, and a boy, Jack, aged five.'

'Lucy, Holly and Jack. Introduce me as Lisa.'

There was the thunder of feet over the wooden floor as he opened the door and shouted, 'I'm home, Ma.' Two fast-moving children threw themselves at him. He picked one up on each arm. Lisa noticed the easy strength with which he did it.

'Now, what have I got?' he asked, kissing the pair.

'Two little bundles of joy,' the boy recited solemnly.

A slim lady in her late fifties now came forward. Lisa thought she was beautiful, but she was also recognisably Alex's mother. It was odd to see a softer version of his stern face. She leaned forward and kissed Alex on the cheek. 'First day all right?' she asked.

'No problem at all. Ma, this is Lisa, who works with me.'

As she shook hands, Lisa was aware that she was being subtly but carefully assessed. She smiled to herself. It was obvious where Alex got some of his characteristics from.

She didn't know how it happened. First she was placed in the living room, and Lucy fetched them all tea. Then Alex went upstairs to change and phone the garage. Lucy excused herself—she had to see to something in the kitchen. Two children stared at her from behind an unwieldy castle, constructed of Lego.

'You can help build it if you want,' Holly said generously. After a while she said, 'In fact, I wish you would.'

Lisa sat cross-legged and clicked in a piece of battlement. She hadn't done anything like this for a while, and it was absorbing. Alex came down in jeans and sweater and squatted opposite her. Before she knew it an hour had passed, and Lucy was asking her to stay for supper.

They ate in the kitchen. Lisa was reminded of the times she'd sat in the kitchen at home with her father, two sisters, and whichever friends happened to be around at the time. They'd had cheerful, noisy meals. She'd enjoyed her own company over the past two years, cooking usually just for herself, but now she remembered what she was missing.

She wasn't allowed to wash up. When she said she had to go it was the family rather than Alex who asked her to call again. Dashing through the rain to her car, she realised she'd thoroughly enjoyed herself.

On the way home, however, reaction set in. Most of her life had been taken up by children—coming to Blazes had been an attempt to start something new. She didn't need more children as friends. She needed... She couldn't force herself to think it.

And Alex was so good with his children—obviously loved them. It made her feel angry at him. Then she was ashamed of her own feelings.

didn't see much of Alex over the following week. was taking time to settle into his new job and, init Sir Arthur being away, there was a lot for him str o.

Marie Pinckney responded well to her medication and regular, well-prepared meals. After a week Lisa could see something of the girl Marie had once been.

'I was taking A levels,' Marie told her. 'I wanted to be an infants teacher. I like little kids.'

'You still could be an infants teacher,' Lisa urged. 'Take an access course and get into college that way.'

The girl shook her head hopelessly. 'You don't do things like that when you've been where I've been. And I know it's all my own fault. Besides, Brian wouldn't let me.'

'You're a free agent. Do what you want.'

But Marie was too weak to argue further, and her eyes closed as she shook her head again.

Lisa decided to have a word with the social worker, although past experience told her it would do little good. Only Marie's personal determination could drag her out of the life she was living.

Brian Barnes came in once or twice, looked surlily at Lisa but said nothing. He didn't stay long. Lisa stayed close to Marie's door while he was in her room.

She had the weekend off again. On Friday night she was restless, not knowing what to do with herself. She kept remembering the previous Saturday night, and the sheer exhilaration of being with Alex.

It struck her that her life was well ordered and happy. She was successful in a job that she enjoyed, but she had nothing whatsoever to look forward ɔ

The phone rang. A childish, rather apprehe᷈ voice said, 'Hello, Lisa, this is Holly Scott.'

Lisa's heart beat a little quicker. 'Nice of ɔ call, Holly. How are you?'

'Well, I've started my new school but I don't like it much. Daddy's doing a barbecue tomorrow night and says I can invite who I like. But I don't know anybody much yet so I'd like to invite you. Can you come?'

Lisa's mind raced. She certainly wasn't doing anything tomorrow night and she'd like to spend time with Lucy, Holly and Jack. They were a nice family. But did she want to spend time with Alex? Yes, she most certainly did. Should she spend time with Alex? That was another question.

Before she could think through the consequences she said, 'I'd love to come to your barbecue Holly.'

'Oh, good!' Then she heard muttering on the other end of the line, and the next voice she heard was Alex's.

'I'm sorry to lumber you with this, Lisa, but I'm a bit soft with the kids sometimes. D'you really want to come? Don't be blackmailed.'

'I won't be blackmailed. Yes, I want to come.'

'About seven, then?' He rang off.

Now she had something to do on her weekend. She wondered still if it was a good idea.

She bought a bottle of wine and a packet of Lego for each of the children. It was a warmish evening, and she dressed comfortably in sweater and trousers. She took some trouble with her hair and make-up, following Sarah's advice. A wicked thought struck her— make sure Alex knows what he's missing.

Holly and Jack greeted her at the door, and her ial apprehension soon faded. She was taken aight to the kitchen, where Lucy accepted her offer of help and said that Alex was outside, getting short-tempered with the barbecue. Would Lisa take this tray of meat out to him and make him wear this pinny?

'Help me put this on the Lego,' Jack said. 'Just for a minute.'

'In exactly ten minutes I will,' Lisa said.

She felt happy. It was good to be part of a family again, with conflicting needs and calls on her time.

She thrilled when she saw Alex. His white T-shirt clung to his muscular body and his jeans emphasised the long lines of his legs. He stood, unconsciously graceful, brooding over the barbecue.

'Why is it, Sister, that I can describe in molecular detail the structure and functions of the liver and yet I can't make these lumps of charcoal glow? Ten thousand years ago men wearing dinosaur skins were doing better than me.'

She peered at the coals. 'You're in too much of a hurry. Wait another few minutes until they turn white at the edges. Then they're ready.'

'Equally expert at bedside or barbecue,' he muttered. 'I hate smart women.'

'Then be a smart man.' She offered him the pinafore Lucy had given her. 'I think the tartan pattern is quite striking.'

He looked at it dubiously. 'I don't really want to wear that. I feel it detracts from my essential masculinity.'

'It won't be your essential masculinity who washes the grease from your shirt,' she said. 'Come on, put it on. Chefs wear aprons.'

'Has ten minutes gone yet?' Jack asked, appearing from nowhere.

'Ten minutes?' Alex queried.

'In ten minutes Lisa's going to help me with my new Lego. Look what she brought.'

His gaze flicked from the packet Jack was holding

to Lisa's face. 'You're good with kids, aren't you?' he asked softly.

'Just had a lot of experience.'

He shouldn't look at her like that with those piercing blue eyes.

There was a verandah at the back of the house, and Holly laid a paper cloth on a table and then brought out plates and bowls of plastic-covered salad. Jack stood with his father and watched the sizzling fat drop onto the coals and flare.

Lisa didn't mind fires outside. She'd had enough barbecues of her own, both with the family and when she'd helped with the Guides. Suddenly there was a glass of red wine in her hand. 'Thanks for the bottle,' Alex said. 'It really is a good choice. Do you drink a lot of this?'

She shook her head. 'I read about it in the Sunday paper and got it from the supermarket. It's supposed to be full-bodied, oaky and rather brash. I thought it would suit you.'

'Ow,' he said. 'I think I'm going to fight back. You've got that interfering look in your eyes. You want to pick up a fork and rearrange my meat and kebabs. Go on, feel free. Rearrange.'

'Well, that sausage is going to fall through.' He was right, but only partly. What she wanted to do was run her hand along the muscles of his back and stroke the powerful arms and shoulders. She'd like that. But instead she rearranged the grilling meat.

It was a good barbecue. Holly ran round making sure every glass was full and everyone had plenty to eat. Lisa felt relaxed. Her initial worries about being so near Alex were partly gone. She felt like one of the family.

She liked Lucy, and the relationship Alex had with her. They were more than mother and son, they were friends. He called her Ma or Lucy, and the children called her Nan.

When most of the meal had been eaten, Holly and Jack dragged Alex into the living room to admire the new Lego, and Lucy and Lisa were left alone.

'D'you like living here?' Lisa asked.

Lucy sighed. 'I miss South Wales and the country-side. But it's easy enough to drive into the country from here. And I love being with the kids—but I miss work.'

'What did you do?' Lisa asked, curiously.

'I was Personnel Manager for an engineering firm. I loved it. But when Sheena went...I mean when I knew the kids would be...'

Lisa realised that Lucy felt uncertain. She was about to talk about Alex's ex-wife and, very properly, knew she shouldn't. But Lisa wanted to know about this Sheena—the woman who'd left her husband and children to go to America. But she couldn't pry.

'I know quite a few places to visit nearby,' she said. 'I'll tell you a few where you can take the kids.'

She saw Lucy smile with relief, and knew she'd recognised and was grateful to Lisa for changing the subject.

It was dark now, though the night was warm. Alex refilled her glass with wine, though he was drinking shandy himself. 'I'm on call,' he explained. Lucy and Lisa carried the dishes through into the kitchen while Alex sent Holly and Jack off for their bath. Then the phone rang.

Alex looked at it with distaste. 'I was enjoying my-self,' he said.

He listened for a while, turned and mouthed at Lisa, 'Hospital'.

'No problem, Paul... Got what? You've done all the tests... I'm sure you have, don't worry... Yes, I'll be right there. I'm glad you called me.'

He turned to a resigned Lucy who said, 'Don't worry, everything is under control here. Off you go.'

Then he turned to Lisa. 'I know it's your weekend off, but there's something quite new turned up. D'you want to come in and have a look?'

Not a lot of nurses would go voluntarily into work on a Saturday evening, Lisa thought, but she was going to. She was always willing to learn. That was the reason she was going, wasn't it?

There were speedy goodbyes to the children and a promise to call again soon. Then Alex went to hospital in his own car and she followed in hers. It seemed odd to walk into her ward when she wasn't in charge, but Ann Pytchley lent her a white coat and she joined Alex and Paul by the side of a comatose patient.

'Good diagnosis, Paul,' Alex was saying. 'Is this the first case you've seen?'

'It is. He was brought in earlier this evening with a history of headache, lethargy and increased tendency to sleep. Things suddenly got worse, and these enlarged glands in the neck suddenly appeared.'

'They're called Winterbottom's sign,' Alex confirmed.

'Well, I took blood and sent it off, and then I talked to the man's wife. Apparently, he's an engineer, been in the Low veld in South Africa for the past six months. That made me wonder—but the blood proved it.'

Alex turned to Lisa and Ann. 'African trypanosomiasis,' he said. 'More popularly known as sleeping
sickness. This poor devil's been bitten by a tsetse fly.'

'What's the treatment?' Ann asked.

'Suramine or pentamidine. They kill one-celled or-
ganisms. With any luck the parasite won't have
reached the brain so we won't need melarsoprol.
That's a drug that penetrates the blood-brain barrier.
But we'll know when we've done more tests. And I
think I'll phone the School of Tropical Medicine.'

Alex turned. 'Well done, Paul. I'll drop in tomorrow to see how he's getting on. You were right to call
me out. Goodnight, Sister.'

Lisa and Alex rode down in the lift together.
'Thank you for the evening,' she said. 'I enjoyed both
parts, if in different ways.'

'Me, too,' he said. 'The trouble is, now I'm all
hyped up. I don't want just to go home and go to bed.
I could almost fancy a walk. Say along the shore.'

The lift doors sighed open. He looked at her ex-
pectantly.

She was tempted, how she was tempted.

'Go home and read a good book,' she advised, and
walked rapidly across the car park.

CHAPTER THREE

DR SCOTT says he'll lend me a book on tropical diseases,' Sarah said as she walked down the ward with Lisa. 'He'll bring it in tomorrow but he wants it back by the weekend. He's nice, isn't he, Lisa?'

'Seems to be a good doctor,' Lisa agreed. 'Why is he lending you this book?'

'I was asking him about our new sleeping sickness case—Mr Ralston. I've never come across anything like it before. Dr Scott goes to a lot of trouble to help us. He's more—approachable than Sir Arthur.'

He certainly is, Lisa thought, but merely said, 'Let me have a glance at the book when you get it.'

The two nurses entered a newly vacated little room and started the automatic process of stripping the bed and remaking it.

'When you first look at him he seems a bit forbidding,' Sarah went on, pulling the sheet tight and tucking it in, 'but when he smiles he's gorgeous. Don't you think so?'

'He's got a gorgeous family. I was round at their house for a barbecue on Saturday night. Two kids and his mother.'

Sarah must have misheard. 'Their mother? What's his wife like?'

'It's his mother, not theirs. He's divorced.'

'That's a pity,' Sarah said. 'D'you know why?'

Lisa did know but wasn't going to say so. 'Just drifted apart, I guess.'

56

'D'you fancy him?' Sarah went on. 'He is attractive in a hunky kind of way. And he's ever so thoughtful.'

'If he's been divorced once he can get divorced again. And I'm not into quick flings.'

Sarah punched her friend lightly on the arm. 'Be a bit forgiving,' she said. 'There are innocent parties, you know. Look at me.'

'I know,' Lisa said. She did know. But sometimes things weren't so simple.

Alex *was* a good doctor. Patients and staff found him more relaxed than Sir Arthur, more easy to talk to—perhaps because he was younger. Lisa knew that she liked working with him. At the moment he was down the ward, talking to Paul. He took his responsibilities towards the junior doctors very seriously. Sir Arthur was good but, since he had so many responsibilities outside the hospital, he always seemed to be busy.

The door was opened and Jeneth, an auxiliary, peered in. She looked worried. 'Sister, could you come and have a look at Marie? She was all right this morning, sitting up and talking to me, but now she's not moving and her pulse is ever so low.'

'I'll come now.' Lisa was already moving down the ward.

One glance at Marie and she knew something was wrong. The patient was lying flat, her face paler than usual, her breathing shallow. 'Ask Dr Scott if he'll come down, will you, Jeneth?' she said tightly. She was pretty sure she knew what had happened, but it wasn't her place to diagnose.

Alex entered. 'Who has—?' he snapped out angrily, then Lisa saw him make a deliberate effort to calm himself. He took Marie's pulse, lifted an eyelid to look at the pinpoint pupil, then turned and looked questioningly at Lisa.

'Jeneth has just reported her condition,' Lisa said. 'All I can say is Marie was fine this morning during the drug round.'

'I see.' He smiled at Jeneth, and Lisa admired the way he made the anxious girl feel she was part of the team. 'We'll have to turn to you for information, Jeneth. What can you tell us?'

'Well, she was all right this morning. I helped her wash and she seemed quite cheerful. Asked me for some magazines—it's the first time she's ever asked for that kind of thing. She had her dinner and then her boyfriend came so I left them alone.'

'Boyfriend,' Alex snarled. 'Some friend he is. Let's look.' Gently he pushed up the sleeves of Marie's gown. Her wasted arms were a sad sight, the collapsed veins easy to see. 'There, I think.' Alex pointed to a tiny ragged puncture mark. 'He's given her an injection—heroin, I'll bet. She had prescription methadone this morning so she's going to be in a hell of a state when she comes down. Her body can't take much more of this kind of treatment. She's undernourished already.'

Jeneth had work to do and left. Alex and Lisa remained at each side of Marie's motionless body. He stroked the thin arm for a moment and then said, 'Lisa, will you tell all staff that the minute that evil little man, Barnes, comes back here they're to phone Security and have him thrown out. And if he breaks his neck—good.'

'I don't think that's the right thing to do,' Lisa said. He looked at her incredulously 'And why not?'

She reminded herself that this was her ward; these

were her charges as well as his. 'I don't think banning him is a good idea,' she repeated. 'D'you want to think about it?'

She'd never seen him angry before. His voice was controlled but icy, and his eyes glittered as they fixed hers. She forced herself to stare back.

'I don't need to think about it. I am her doctor, Sister, and I expect you to follow my directions as to her medical care.'

'She is also in nursing care. For twenty-four hours a day.'

There was silence as they glared at each other. Then he said, 'That is, of course, true. Please tell me what you think.'

Shakily she marshalled her arguments. 'I dislike Barnes as much as you do but Marie's got social and psychological problems, as well as medical ones. Barnes is all she's got—he and drugs are her life. He gives her drugs, steals her money and sometimes beats her. She's tried to leave him—but she always comes back.'

Alex's expression had changed. She could tell he was still angry, but at least he was listening. 'Go on,' he said. 'Surely the thing to do is to try to separate her from Barnes?'

'She has to decide to do that—not us. If we stop him coming she'll fret and she'll worry and the minute she's capable of doing so she'll sign herself out. Any good we've done so far will be ruined.'

He frowned again, then gave a thin smile. I've convinced him, Lisa thought. Well, almost.

'You may well be right. But can you ensure that when and if Barnes comes in again there's no chance of this happening again?' He paused a moment and then went on, 'That is in no way a reflection on your nursing care.'

'I'll see that she's chaperoned,' Lisa promised. 'There'll be no problem there.'

'And when he does come in next will you bleep me?'

She looked at him dubiously. 'Are you sure that's a good idea?'

'Possibly not,' he said ironically, 'but, as you know, Sister, dealing sympathetically with family and friends is part of a doctor's job.'

'Quite,' she said.

'Don't worry, I'll be proper and professional, but someone's got to say something, you do see that.'

Suddenly he smiled, unexpected in that fraught atmosphere. She had to smile back—she couldn't help herself. He could move her so easily.

'What are we arguing about, Lisa?' he asked. 'We're friends. Why don't you do what Lucy does after an argument?'

'I can guess,' she said drily. 'Go and put on the kettle. I'll see you in my office.'

Shakily she went to do as he had suggested as she needed a drink herself. She thought she was right—but she'd been shocked at how much Alex's disapproval had hurt her. He's getting too close to me, she thought.

She had just poured the two teas when he rejoined her. He accepted his cup and then said, 'Lisa, I'm sorry if I lost my temper. I had a case like Marie in my last hospital—a young lad. I thought I'd done a good job on him. He was pulling through when his mates brought him something to sniff. He died on the ward, his heart just couldn't take it. You'll forgive me?'

'Of course I'll forgive you. After all, I'm getting plenty of practice.'

He shook his head. 'I'm glad you're not a boxer,' he said. 'You'd be a really dirty fighter.'

'I'll take that as a compliment. Listen, Alex, are you the right man to speak to Barnes? The head of Security is a good man—he's an ex-policeman. He'd do it.'

He smiled. 'Don't worry Lisa, I won't lose my temper, I promise. But bleep me when he comes.'

She said she would.

Lisa thought about the morning's happenings quite a lot through the day. Alex's behaviour had been a little surprising. So far on the ward he'd been a model of courteous behaviour, thoughtful with patients and staff alike. Even Sir Arthur had been known to snap at times, but Alex never did. When someone did something wrong Alex corrected them politely.

With a tiny shiver she realised that there was another dimension to him. He was capable of passion, of raw emotion. And the fact that he usually had enough self-control to rein it in only made it more disturbing.

Brian Barnes came onto the ward again late that afternoon. He didn't seem anxious. There was even a cockiness in his walk. For a moment Lisa hesitated—should she send for Security? Then she decided against it. Alex could make his own decisions. She bleeped him. Then, managing an artificial smile, she asked Barnes into her office.

'The doctor in charge of Miss Pinckney needs to talk to you. I'm afraid she'd had a bit of a relapse.'

He didn't seem too worried. 'She'll be OK. She'd had this kind of trouble before. But if I'm waiting is there any chance of a coffee?'

Lisa kept calm and said nothing. Though it hurt.

Seconds later Alex strode in. His face was a little paler than usual, and the smile that flicked across it would have fooled nobody.

'Hi, Doc,' Barnes said, not standing but offering a hand.

Alex ignored the hand. 'Mr Barnes, I wanted to speak to you,' he said silkily. 'You came onto the ward this morning and injected one of my patients with heroin.'

Barnes was not expecting such a frontal attack, but he tried to fight back. 'Marie's an addict, you know that. She's got to have drugs, and you're just not giving her enough.'

'She's showing signs of recovering from hepatitis. I'm not willing to discuss the details of her treatment with you. I just want to tell you one thing. You could have killed her today. Injecting with a dirty needle is bad enough, but at this stage of her treatment it could have been fatal.'

Barnes flushed. 'Come on, Doc, I've more experience of this kind of drugs than you have. I know what she can stand.'

Lisa thought he seemed genuinely upset by the accusation. Perhaps he had a touch of real regard for poor Marie.

Alex, however, hadn't finished. 'You do not have more experience than I. She might have died. She still might, it's not impossible. If she does you will be charged with her manslaughter. I'll see to that.'

He stood and leaned over Barnes's chair, forcing the man to cower. His voice was a rasping snarl. 'In this ward *I* direct all the drugs. Any interference with my patient and you will take the consequences. Is that clear? I said—is that clear?'

'Yes…it's clear.'

'Good.' Mysteriously Alex's voice had returned to its normal good-humoured tones. 'Mr Barnes may see his friend now, Sister. Just for a while. Don't let him close the door.'

'No, Doctor.' Lisa led Barnes out of her office. He seemed glad to escape.

'I think you frightened him,' she said when she returned. 'You certainly frightened me.'

'I doubt it in both cases,' he said wearily, 'but I hope it did some good. The trouble with addicts is that you make some impression—think they're going to pull through—and then their friends drag them down. I know we're supposed to keep our distance, not get involved, but it angers me.'

She wondered again about him when he was gone. So far he'd been the ideal caring doctor, a man who never cut corners. This ruthlessness showed a new side of him. He'd been, well, almost unprofessional. She thought she liked it.

Three days later, on Thursday, Lisa didn't go straight home. Instead, she had a shower, changed into a smart blue dress and waited in the foyer downstairs. A burly man in a dark uniform saw her and doubled back.

'Sister Grey. I wanted to talk to you.'

She smiled at Ben Holt, the head of Security.

'Hello, Ben. Not parking in the wrong place again, am I?'

He laughed. 'Nothing's more serious than parking in this hospital. No, it's just that I had a word with Dr Scott a couple of days ago. He says you've had some trouble with a Brian Barnes.'

'Not recently,' she said cautiously. 'He's kept a low profile.'

She was rather pleased that Alex had spoken to Security. The thought nagged her that Barnes was likely to do something stupid again.

'Well, I've kept in touch with a few friends on the force and I asked about Barnes. Not a pleasant man at all. They think he's into dealing but nothing's been pinned on him yet. If there's any more trouble I think you ought to let us know.'

'Have you told Dr Scott that?'

'Yes. He agrees with me. Now, be careful where you park in future.' With a laugh, Ben moved on.

It was interesting, she thought, that Alex had followed her advice and spoken to Security. She wondered if— Then she saw a gold-painted Jaguar stop in the car park, and set off smartly to meet it.

Before she was out of the doors she heard a woman behind her say, 'Look, that's Harry Shea—you know, out of *Redstone*. Isn't he big?'

It didn't take Lisa long to reach the car but, even so, a couple were there before her, collecting an autograph. They looked up cautiously.

Harry Shea was big—about six feet four—and had a wrestler's build to go with it. With his shaved head and thick black moustache he looked villainous. The suit doesn't help, Lisa thought gloomily. It was some kind of shiny silver grey material, and was matched with a black tieless shirt.

Harry saw her coming, and his habitually scowling face lit up. He grabbed her, lifted her bodily in the air and kissed her.

'Put me down,' Lisa whispered. 'I work here.' She was aware of the curious faces of the onlookers.

Harry put her down and said, 'This is Sister Grey, the best nurse in the hospital. She nursed my father. I'm pleased you enjoy the show, it's great fun making it.'

Then Lisa was swiftly eased into the Jaguar and it pulled away.

'I don't think I want you telling people I'm the best nurse in the hospital,' Lisa said after a while. 'Not only is it not true, but what happens if people come in and ask for me?'

Harry shrugged. 'I think it's true. And I think people ought to try to get the best. Let them ask for you.'

'The very thought frightens me,' she muttered. 'Harry, tell me who your tailor is. I must remember to avoid him.'

'This suit is a bit lurid, isn't it?' he said with some satisfaction. 'I'll not tell you what it cost—you might hit me—but it does the job. This is *the* suit for a television villain.'

'Put that way, I suppose you're right,' she said with a sigh. 'D'you have to play a villain outside the studio?'

'Why not? Do you stop being a nurse when you take off your uniform?'

'It's not the same.' She had noticed the attitude of the couple who had asked for the autograph—fascinated but a bit apprehensive. 'Too many people can't tell the difference between life and television.'

'Thank goodness for that,' Harry said comfortably.

Redstone Park was a television soap opera filmed on the far side of the city, based on houses around an old park. It was famous for dealing with topics other television series shied away from. Lisa had watched the odd episode, and had to admit that it dealt with drug-taking with brutal clarity.

Harry Shea played Mick Mort, a drug dealer and club owner. As he had once told Lisa, 'I don't play Mick Mort, I overplay him. There's nothing the British public like better than a big bad wolf.'

'I saw your picture in the paper last week,' Lisa said interestedly. 'With a blonde girl. She said she was expecting to make a statement about the pair of you in a week or two. What happened to her?'

When Harry wasn't acting, or opening fêtes or supermarkets for a considerable fee, he was usually being photographed, coming out of a nightclub with a girl half his age on his arm.

Now he scowled. 'The one with lots of hair, teeth and bosom?'

'That describes most of them,' Lisa said cattily.

'True. Well, I knew this one wasn't very bright— but just how dim I never suspected. She wanted to work in show business but she didn't know how to handle the Press. She was in last week's papers. She won't be in next week's.'

'So ends a career,' Lisa said.

Harry patted her affectionately on the thigh. 'But why should I worry about her? After all, I've got you—and who could ask for anything more?'

'Get your hand off my leg,' Lisa snapped. 'And you haven't got me. Though you tried hard enough.'

'Sorry, Lisa,' Harry said, obviously meaning it. He turned to her, worried. 'We weren't going to mention my earlier behaviour. It's not like you. Are you having any sort of a bad time?'

She had to warm to his obvious concern. 'Something like that,' she mumbled, 'but it's my own fault. I'll tell you about it later.'

'Just relax then.' He leaned forward and switched on the car stereo. Once she'd told him how much she enjoyed Ella Fitzgerald. It was typical of him that he'd bought two of her CDs and always kept them in the car. Now the sad tones of 'Stormy Weather' filled the car. She wondered if they were prophetic.

Six months ago an old man called Lennie Shackleton had been brought onto the ward, suffering from pneumonia. He had lived on his own in a tiny terraced house in the centre of town. His life had revolved around the local pub which he'd visited every lunchtime and evening.

Typically he'd only come into hospital when he'd collapsed there. Lisa had examined the brown-stained fingers and looked at the grey face wrenched with coughing.

'No more smoking for you for a while, Lennie. It's killing you.'

'Smoked for sixty years,' the pained voice wheezed. 'Too late to stop now.'

There was a grin on his face but she recognised it for what it was. Lennie was afraid.

Sir Arthur was worried. He looked at the cyanosis on Lennie's lips and nails, the tell-tale blueness that suggested poor oxygen supply. Lennie was complaining of pleuritic pain. His chest hurt, and there was limited movement down one side. A specimen of sputum had been taken and sent down to the lab so the microbiologists could culture and identify the organism causing the disease.

'It's going to be twenty-four hours before the lab comes up with a firm identification,' Sir Arthur told Lisa, 'but I'm pretty sure this is a viral complication of chronic bronchitis. We'll treat him with a broad-spectrum antibiotic. Ampicillin, I think.'

Lisa nodded. Sir Arthur went on, 'You know it'll be a while before the drug has any effect. His survival over the next couple of days will depend upon his nursing as much as his medical care.'

For the next forty-eight hours Lennie managed to hang on. Lisa ordered hot-water bottles placed next to his chest to relieve the pain in breathing. When his temperature spiked Lennie was cooled by sponging with tepid water. He was coaxed to eat—light but nourishing soup. And slowly he pulled round.

When Lennie finally felt better the real battle began. He forgot how ill he had been, and saw no reason why he shouldn't live the way he'd been living before. A tussle of wills started—over food, drink, smoking. And slowly Lisa won.

It happened some time later when Lennie was well on the way to recovery. She heard whispered words outside her office.

'It *is* him!'

'What's he doing here?'

'He's just like he is on...'

Then the door of her office was pushed open and a vast man walked in. He was dressed in a dark raincoat and gave out an aura of menace.

'I gather my father is here, seriously ill. Why wasn't I told?'

Vaguely Lisa thought she recognised the man. She certainly recognised the attitude. A lot of people were defensive about their care of their parents. 'And you are?' she asked icily.

'Lennie Shackleton is my father.'

'I see. With a man of your father's age and condition, we are particularly keen to get in touch with relations. I've spoken to Mr Shackleton several times. He's stated emphatically that he has no next of kin except his son, who is abroad. He didn't know where his son was, his son never came to visit him and we were not to bother him.'

'The awkward, lying old devil. I've just looked in his room, Sister. He's asleep but he doesn't look too good. May I sit down?'

There was a queer mixture of emotions on the man's face. There was affection and concern certainly, but also exasperation.

'Your father has been very ill. He'll have to change his lifestyle.'

'You persuade him—I can't. I've offered to buy him a new flat, get him a place in sheltered accommodation, even put central heating in that shack he lives in. When I leave money for him on the mantelpiece it's still there under the clock a week later.'

'So you do visit him?'

'Of course I do. At least once a week, usually more often. I've been abroad for fortnight but I left him my hotel address.'

Lisa decided the man was telling the truth. In fact, she rather liked him. And his description of Lennie's character rang true. 'We'll go and see your father now. If you come for a chat afterwards, we'll see what we can do about when he leaves. Er...do I know you?'

A laugh rumbled in the man's throat. 'I'm better known as Harry Shea.'

Lisa looked at him, with polite incomprehension.

'You're good for my self-esteem, Sister. I act on television in a programme called "Redstone Park". I'm supposed to be quite well known.'

'Sorry,' Lisa mumbled.

After that Harry was in every day. He saw what Lisa was managing to do—she was better with Lennie than he was. It was Lisa who finally persuaded Lennie to take a place in sheltered accommodation in a house where he could see and hear the ships on the river. Lennie had been a sailor.

Harry was genuinely grateful. He persuaded Lisa to go to dinner with him as a gesture of gratitude. They had a meal in an expensive restaurant, then he drove her to a quiet park, put his arm round her and kissed her confidently.

Lisa had been warned about his reputation. 'That's it, Harry, one kiss. I'm not one of your little pals. Now take me straight home.'

Harry obviously thought she was joking, and made no attempt to move off. Lisa leaned forward, took the keys and held them out of the car window. 'Do we drive back now, Harry, or do I throw these keys in that pond?'

There was silence in the car. Then Harry laughed. 'I'll take you home. Give me the keys back.' And he drove her home. Next day a great bunch of carnations was delivered, with a note saying, 'From a friend, not a lover.'

They became friends. They went out about once a month, and she enjoyed his company. She even enjoyed the fact that no one quite understood their relationship.

On this particular evening Harry took her to a pub on the moors where they could have a pleasant meal and not be disturbed. They gossiped, and talked about his father. Then, as he cut into his steak, he asked her what was bothering her. Since there was nothing sexual between them they could talk together as friends. Lisa liked talking to him. He was the exact opposite of the cunning criminal he played on screen.

'I've found a man I could really go for, Harry,' she said. 'I like him a lot.'

'Lucky man. Tell me about him.'

She described Alex—what he looked like, how she enjoyed working with him, the way she'd met him.

'So what's the problem? He must like you, no man couldn't.'

'He's been married, Harry, has two kids. His ex-wife's away studying in America.'

'Then everything is clear for you.'

'He's had enough of long-term relationships,' Lisa said glumly. 'He's not prepared to commit himself.'

'And you're not interested in anything less?'

'I'd give him time, but you know how I feel. For me there's got to be at least the chance of...well, something lasting.'

'And he just wants to have an affair with you? Short and sweet, no strings attached.'

'I think that's it, Harry. But he's been fair with me. I know what he wants but he hasn't pushed me.'

'Are you going to have an affair with him?'

That was the question. Desperately she sought for

an honest answer. 'I just don't know, Harry. Some of me wants to but I know I shouldn't, that it wouldn't be good for me.'

'Yes, I know.' He leaned over and patted her shoulder, genuinely worried for her. 'I can't offer any advice. Only you can sort this out. But remember, Lisa, if you live with him you'll have to live with yourself as well.'

'I know. And I couldn't.' It was as simple as that.

'Now,' she said, 'that's enough high drama. Tell me more about the show. Is it true about Aubrey Williams and Ann Dent?'

Harry grinned. He loved to gossip, and he'd found out that anything he told Lisa stayed firmly with her. 'Well,' he said, 'when I saw them last Monday...'

They both enjoyed their evening, but Harry brought her back quite early. Television was a hard taskmaster and he had to be up at some ridiculous hour to film the next day. 'Just like nursing,' she teased.

'Not really. Nursing is harder and the money's much worse.'

Outside her flat he kissed her on the cheek and promised to keep in touch. 'Stick to what you know is right,' he called after her. 'You'll be better for it.'

'Ten million fans of Mick Mort wouldn't agree with you,' she quipped, and walked to her flat. She liked Harry, and felt better for their talk.

There was a light on in her flat, and Lisa frowned a little. She knew who it would be—her sister Rosalind had a key. Normally Rosalind stayed in her own room in the town centre hospital during the week, only visiting at weekends.

She was sitting cross-legged on Lisa's couch, a small figure in black jeans and sweater. Only the distinctive rich auburn hair showed her to be a relation. In front of her on the coffee table were notes, texts and papers. There was a glass of milk on a coaster. Rosalind brought neatness with her as other people attracted chaos.

She stood as Lisa entered, and the two sisters hugged each other. It was a family tradition. They didn't kiss each other much but they hugged a lot. Lisa remembered the many times she'd held Rosalind's tight little body. This time she felt the tension in it which, as ever, drained away as Rosalind relaxed.

'I'll make you some tea,' Rosalind said. 'It's all ready.'

Lisa wanted to ask questions but she knew it was foolish. Her sister only did things in her own time. Carefully Rosalind packed her bag with what was on the table and then fetched the tray with the tea. She poured two cups.

'I had a phone call from Chile earlier today,' she said abruptly. 'From Jack Coles, a friend of Dad's. Dad went trekking up into the mountains with a group last week. He hasn't come back. Apparently the entire group has disappeared.'

Lisa blinked, unable to take this in. Rosalind's calm voice only made things seem worse. 'You mean... they're lost or something? Has there been a storm and they're marooned somewhere? Some kind of natural disaster?'

'Jack says it's nothing like that. The countryside's quite pleasant, no natural dangers in it. Jack thinks they might be being held by the locals.'

'But why?' Lisa was hardly able to credit this. 'Dad's never been a danger to anyone.'

Rosalind shrugged. 'Who can tell? But Jack says these things usually sort themselves out. We shouldn't worry. He only let me know because he didn't want us to learn about it from anyone else.'

'What do we do?'

'We do nothing until we have further information. You know what Dad would want. He'd want us not to worry.'

'I know he would. But it's easier to say than to do.'

With her habitual economy of movement Rosalind stood and swung her bag on her shoulder. 'I'll phone for a taxi and go now. If there's any news I'll ring you at once. Bye, love, don't worry.'

But they both knew that they both would.

My private life is getting too chaotic, Lisa thought on the ward next day, but at least I can forget things at work. There are always problems here.

She had to have a word with Marie about the dangers she ran, taking drugs while still being treated for hepatitis. For the past few days Marie's condition had been so bad that any logical conversation had been impossible. Lisa thought this was just the time that Barnes might bring her more in.

Marie was alternatively tearful and truculent. 'Brian says we pay our taxes, and it's nothing to do with you what I choose to take. Your job is to get me better.'

Lisa wondered how long it had been since either Marie or Barnes had paid taxes, but she contented herself with saying, 'We're doing the best we can do to cure you, Marie. But heroin won't help. In fact, it's likely to kill you.'

Then Marie felt sorry—either for what she'd done or for herself. 'I didn't mean to be nasty, Lisa, you know that. I just feel terrible. And you don't give me enough. One dose of methadone a day just won't do. Can't I have an extra dose? Just for today? I promise I won't ask again.'

'No. You know the rules,' Lisa said wearily.

'Oh, get out of my room! You make me sick, all of you.'

There was one thing to be said for drug addicts. They were predictable.

It was a treat to walk back into her office and find Alex, waiting for her. When he smiled her heart lurched, and she wondered if what he was doing to her was good for her. It certainly felt good.

'Lisa, have you got any plans for tomorrow?' he asked.

She looked at him warily. She'd enjoyed the barbecue last weekend but she wasn't sure she wanted to go back to his house. Well, not yet. 'There's nothing I couldn't put off,' she said.

He pulled a paper from his briefcase and handed it to her. 'I'm going over the Pennines tomorrow, there's this lecture on tropical infectious diseases and their spread into Europe. I know the speaker—he's good. Would you like to come?'

She looked at the programme. It seemed very interesting. Over the past twenty years, with so much travel and immigration, many diseases which had once been confined to the tropics were now finding their way to Britain. Last week's case of trypanosomiasis was one example, but she knew of cases of malaria, the itchiness and painful muscles of dengue fever, even the ulcers that suggested yaws.

'I'd like to come,' she said. 'You can never learn too much.'

'Right, then. Look, pack a change of clothing and a pair of boots and we'll go for a walk on the way back. Pick you up at seven in the morning?'

Things were all going a bit too fast, but now she was swept up in it. 'All right,' she said. 'I'm looking forward to it.' She was looking forward to spending a day with him. That was the trouble.

CHAPTER FOUR

LISA took out her walking kit that night, as well as something more suitable for the conference. She was looking forward to tomorrow and not, she had to admit, because she expected to learn something. She was going to spend the day with Alex. She'd seen quite a lot of him, but had not really been on her own with him since that magic evening they'd first met. And look what the result of that was, she thought. She wondered how the day would go, how she'd feel at the end of it. Was she just teasing herself?

It was late when her doorbell rang. She was ready to go to bed. Rosalind stood there, her face as expressionless as ever. But when they gave each other the ritual hug Lisa could tell that something was wrong.

'It's Dad,' she said.

'Too important to phone. I've just heard from Jack Coles. Some of the people trekking with Dad have turned up. But not him. He's been kidnapped by guerillas.'

'He's what?' Lisa gasped.

'Been kidnapped by guerillas. A band called Dark Sky, Fast River, apparently. Funny how they give themselves such imaginative names, isn't it?'

'Never mind the name!' Lisa screamed. 'Don't you ever get upset?'

'No,' said Rosalind.

Lisa reminded herself not to get angry. She knew

Rosalind of old. Whenever she was upset she faced the problem by retiring into an icy calmness. People who didn't know her well found it disquieting in the extreme. Only a few knew the depth of feeling under the cold exterior.

'What else did Jack Coles say?'

'He feels there's no reason to worry yet. They've kidnapped foreigners before and usually look after them very well. They're trying to force concessions out of the government. They hope foreign governments will bring pressure to bear if they kidnap the odd tourist.'

'So Dad's just a pawn in someone else's fight?'

'Exactly. The people who were with him said he was quite comfortable and happy, and that he'd made friends with a couple of the bandits.'

'I might have guessed,' Lisa muttered. Her father's capacity for making friends was unrivalled. 'What do we do now?'

'Jack Coles is getting in touch with the local embassy and they'll get in touch with the Foreign Office. Then we just wait.'

'Great. What do we do about Emily?' Their other sister was a midwife in Africa.

'Well, we'll have to tell her,' Rosalind said firmly. 'I'll write and make it seem like something not very important, otherwise she's likely to fly to Chile and start her own war.'

'That's true,' Lisa said.

'And publicity is the last thing we need. Jack Coles says that it'll all be sorted out by local negotiation. Publicity would force the two sides into making statements they can't back away from. Come on, Lisa, don't be upset.'

'That's easy for you to say.'

There was a pause, and then Rosalind said, 'Hey, you're the oldest sister. For a while you're the head of the family. So look after us.'

'I will,' said Lisa. 'If I can. Are you going to stay the night?'

'No. Work to do tomorrow. Give me another hug, head of family. Remember what Dad would want us do. He's probably thoroughly enjoying himself.' Then she was gone.

Lisa knew Rosalind was right. For her father's sake she shouldn't worry. But it was hard. She had a long hot bath, tried to read, even had a small glass of the brandy she kept strictly for medicinal reasons. None of it worked. It was hours before she slept.

For Lisa it was unheard of. She overslept. When the doorbell rang next morning she was still bleary-eyed and in her dressing-gown, knowing her hair needed a good brushing.

It didn't help when Alex appeared, looking wondrously elegant in medical conference uniform—a dark suit, white shirt and silk tie, this time in a burgundy shade.

'Sorry I'm late. Come in and I'll get you a quick coffee,' she mumbled. 'Or if you don't want to wait you can go without me.'

'I'm happy to wait, and why don't I make coffee for both of us?' he said urbanely. 'You get showered and you'll feel better. Then you can tell me what's wrong.'

'How d'you know something's wrong?' she asked suspiciously.

'I've never known you late for anything. You run the ward like clockwork. I know something's wrong.'

'It must be lovely to be as clever as you.'

But when she was showered and dressed in the grey suit she used for formal meetings she realised she did feel better. Then she put on her gold wrist-watch, realised it was a twenty-first present from her father and felt worse again.

She had carefully avoided thinking about the clinking noises coming from her tiny kitchen, but was still surprised when she found he'd made coffee for two and toast and marmalade for her—neatly set out on the kitchen table.

'Marry me and we'll eat like this every morning,' she said, and then blushed. 'Sorry, that wasn't necessary.'

But Alex didn't seem to mind. 'Best offer I've had this week,' he said. 'Now, I know this is how you like your coffee so drink it and tell me what's wrong.' After a pause he said, 'If you want to, that is.'

She sighed, sat down and decided she did want to tell him. 'You know I told you about my father always wanting to travel in South America?'

'I remember very well.'

'Well, it looks like he's…' It was surprisingly easy to tell him what Rosalind had told her. He was a good listener, and even came round the table and put his arm round her shoulders in a non-threatening way. He said, 'I'd like to meet your father some day, and I'm sure I will. I know it's easy to deal with other people's troubles but for now your sister is right. Think of what he'd want you to do.'

So she did. And after that things were easier. She was glad she'd told him.

The morning picked up as they drove away. It was going to be a glorious day. Alex's new car had now been delivered and she looked with approval at the sleek lines of the blue Mondeo. They were quickly out of town and on the motorway that led to the Pennines.

'Where's the family?' she asked.

'Gone away for the weekend. Visiting my brother, Mike, who's a GP down in Gloucestershire. I put them on the train last night.'

'Did you ever want to be a GP?'

He thought for a minute. 'Not really, although I can see the attraction. When I stay with him I help out a bit on his rounds, I like it that he knows everybody. But he has to send his serious cases to hospital and I like to follow things through.'

'Gloucestershire. Isn't that near your old hospital?'

'Quite near.'

'It's nice there. I've been through once or twice. Don't you find this industrial landscape a bit different?'

She thought for a moment that his face hardened, but his voice was pleasant as he said, 'I'm thirty-six. I'd been there a long time. There was a danger of getting stuck in my ways, and it was the right time for the kids to move. Didn't you feel the same way, leaving Shropshire?'

'Entirely the same way,' she agreed.

She had him on her own for a while and she couldn't help herself. 'Did you leave to try to forget your wife?'

His voice remained as cordial as ever, but she felt he didn't enjoy answering her question. 'I suppose that's possible. We'd largely forgotten her anyway.'

'*We'd* forgotten her?'

'The children. Well, Holly.' Now she could tell he was angry—but not, she felt, at her.

'Did her leaving upset you much?'

'At first, yes, but it was a gradual thing—a slow realisation. I loved her, you see—or I thought I loved her. And I thought she loved me. Perhaps she did in her own way.'

Lisa was half-sorry she had brought up the subject, but she was still fascinated by what he had said. After a pause she said, 'I'm sorry about the inquisition. I can't say I didn't want to pry, because I suppose I did.'

Her artless reply made him laugh. 'I think I'm glad you're interested in me, Lisa. Shall I tell you about it?'

'I'd like to hear it if you'd like to tell me.'

He seemed preoccupied, and didn't speak for a while. Then he said sardonically, 'It's a short story. I don't know who comes out worst in it—my ex-wife or myself.'

'It might be your children who suffer most,' Lisa couldn't help pointing out.

He winced. 'One of the things I like about you, Lisa, is how you've turned honesty into an instrument of torture. You're right. The children must come first.

'I first met Sheena when she was a medical student in her final year and I was a junior registrar, doing a bit of teaching. She was six years younger than me.'

As she looked at his troubled face Lisa wondered if she wanted him to go on. Certainly she was interested, fascinated even. But, for her, would this be good news or bad?

'I was impressed by Sheena. She was by no means

my brightest pupil, but she was calm, methodical, a very hard worker. She always did well in exams because she prepared well. Better students than her did worse. She was never shy about asking for help, and I gave her a lot of extra tuition. And one night she just didn't leave my flat. A year later, after she qualified, we got married.'

It doesn't sound like the love affair of the century, Lisa thought, but she said nothing.

'It was typical of her that she didn't want a big wedding. Too much fuss about nothing, she said. Lucy was a bit upset. Mike had had a big ceremony in his home village and she'd enjoyed it. But we got it over with and carried on with our careers. We were both very busy. I suppose we were happy enough, though it sometimes seemed more like a partnership than a wedding.

'Then Holly arrived, quite quickly. I wanted Sheena to take at least a year off, but she wouldn't hear of it. She was back working full time within two months. The same thing happened with Jack. She felt she couldn't leave her studies. By now she was specialising in plastic surgery. Then she had this opportunity to work in America—it was a wonderful career move. She didn't even talk to me, before accepting.'

'Did she keep in touch?'

He shrugged. 'She never liked writing letters. For a while she phoned once a week. But then she was too busy. After a year I flew over to talk to her. She just said her work was important, she couldn't leave it now. When I got back I stopped trying to keep her in the kids' minds. As a mother she was worse than useless. Then a letter arrived, suggesting divorce. And I jumped at it.'

He turned to her, and his smile was strained. 'So, that's my story. I'm now not a married man, I'm fancy-free.'

'You're not free, you're wounded,' Lisa said.

He shook his head. 'I made a mistake with a woman. I shan't do it again. Any further relationship I form will be light-hearted—casual even.'

'Not all women are alike,' Lisa said desperately.

'I know that. But how do you tell in advance? I've been wrong about love once already. To make the same mistake twice would be foolish.'

'I suppose that's a point,' she said miserably.

They had crossed the coastal plain and were now swinging up the green slopes of the Pennines. Long vistas of hills opened up in front of them. To break the silence Lisa said, 'I get carried away, asking questions, sometimes. Don't you find this when you're interviewing patients?'

There was more enthusiasm in his voice when he answered. She realised how pleased he was that the subject had been changed. He said, 'Any young student can learn how to use a stethoscope or sphygmomanometer, but real medical skill lies in questioning patients. I sometimes wonder if I'm a doctor or a social worker, or even a policeman. Especially with infectious diseases.'

A reflective smile played on his face, and she could tell he was thinking of something. 'I had a case of salmonella poisoning once, an old lady. She was in a bad way and we had to give her antispasmodics to deal with her diarrhoea, and transfusions to get her lost fluids up. I thought we'd lose her, but she was a tough old girl.

'Then we tried to find out the cause. That was really

troublesome. It turned out she was once a nurse her-self. The old type of nurse. The district nurse who looked round her cottage said it was spotless. You could have performed an operation on her kitchen ta-ble. So when I suggested food poisoning there was a really big row. Food poisoning to her meant dirt or, even worse, stupidity.'

Lisa was fascinated by this story. It was like so many she'd come across herself. 'Go on,' she said. 'What did you find out?'

He laughed. 'It was daft, really. She told me she was worried about the cottage getting dirty while she was away—but at least the garden was all right and the windows had just been cleaned. For some reason I asked her about the window cleaners. They'd asked her to heat water for their tea. When they'd finished, they left half a bottle of milk on a window-sill. It had been in the sun all day when she found it and put it in her fridge. That night she absent-mindedly took some for her tea. She'd completely forgotten about it when the disease hit her.'

The two of them laughed. Lisa knew that one of the commonest causes of food poisoning was dairy products that had been allowed to get warm and then cooled again.

Alex went on to talk about the lecture they were going to hear—he'd heard Professor Rodney Starrat before, and he was a very good speaker. They chatted about the foreign diseases they'd come across. Between them they'd come across blackwater fever, dengue fever, malaria, leishmaniasis. He'd come across a case of leprosy, and once even a case of suspected cholera. That had really upset the hospital he was working in.

*   *   *

The lecture was very good and, although it was principally aimed at doctors and medical officers of health, Lisa picked up a few tips about nursing. As always, she scribbled down what she wanted to remember, but at the end she was given a handsome folder with notes and pictures. Afterwards there was a short reception in a panelled hall.

'Now you're to leave me here and talk to other people,' Lisa told Alex. 'I don't want to be dragged round and introduced. It'll stop you networking.'

'But I'm proud of my ward Sister! And I don't network.'

'Everyone in medicines networks,' she told him. 'It's part of the job.' For a moment the Blazes Ball flashed across her mind, but she didn't mention it. 'Anyway, I want to network on my own, which I can't do with you hanging over my shoulder. I might get a better job.'

'Don't even think about it! I'll fetch you something from the buffet and—'

'I can feed myself. Now, off you go.'

He surveyed her in silence for a moment, and she realised he appreciated what she was doing. 'Go on,' she said softly.

She felt happy in the dignified room, surrounded by groups of softly speaking professionals. After a while she found herself in conversation with an older man, who looked at her name badge and asked her how she had enjoyed the lecture. She explained how interesting she'd found it—if a little alarming.

'Diseases that only fifteen years ago would have seemed mysterious and outlandish are now becoming common,' she said. 'In the past two years I've had to deal with two cases of schistosomiasis—one of them led to kidney failure. And yet a sixty-year-old staff nurse who works with me had never seen a case before in her life.'

Lisa shuddered. All diseases were unpleasant, but the idea of a fluke penetrating the skin of a swimmer, and then laying its eggs in the bloodstream, seemed more unpleasant than most.

The old man nodded. 'Fortunately, it's very easy to treat with praziquantel—always supposing it is diagnosed in time. Then all we need is dedicated nursing. Tell me, do you find any special problems, nursing tropical diseases?' He seemed very interested in the little she could tell him. Then they were politely interrupted.

'Professor Williams, have you a moment?'

The man who had given the lecture, Rodney Starrat, came over, and with a smile the old man excused himself. 'It's been nice talking to you, my dear.'

The crowd was now thinning. Lisa had kept her eye on Alex. He seemed to be both well known and popular, and many people came up to speak to him. But now he came back to reclaim her.

'I saw you talking to Professor Williams,' he said.

'He seemed very pleasant. Asked me about nursing tropical diseases.'

'Professor Owen Williams. Only two other men in the country know as much as he does about tropical diseases.'

'I hope he found my contribution interesting,' she murmured.

They were walking to his car as they talked, and she needed an answer to something that had been puzzling her. 'That wasn't a public lecture. Someone must have paid for me. Did you?'

He opened the car door for her. 'Yes, I did. I thought it something the ward sister should hear.'

'Well, I did enjoy it but I must pay—'

'What you must do is accept gracefully. Bringing you here will make my job easier. Now don't mention it again.' He walked to his own side of the car.

As he got in she said, 'But—'

'No. Now pass me the road atlas.'

She decided to say no more.

It was only two o'clock when they got to the first motorway café. Alex suggested that they changed clothes there. She looked at him with approval as he reappeared. His boots, breeches, wool shirt and Bergen anorak were all expensive but well used. Like her own kit, in fact.

He had looked the perfect urbane doctor in his dark suit. Now he looked the perfect outdoor man. He smiled at her and said, 'Walking gear suits you, Lisa.' She felt a shiver of pure delight. This man could move her so easily!

'Can you navigate?' he asked as they turned off the motorway into the moors of Derbyshire.

'I can.'

'Then find us a route to here.' He pointed out their destination in the atlas. After that he followed her instructions, as she took him along a maze of tiny roads, most with entrancing views.

'Where are we going?' she asked after a while.

'Holly wants some fossils to take to school. One of the doctors told me where they could be found.'

'Turn right down here, then.' She took him down a narrow dead-end road to park by a Forestry

Commission plantation. Then they started to walk up a broad river valley.

They met no other walkers. Eventually the valley closed in on them and the path clung to the valley side, high above the river. Lisa was enjoying herself, feeling her heartbeat rise as they climbed, stretching her legs in the unaccustomed exercise. The path was narrow, and she was following Alex who was obviously an experienced walker. She looked at the easily swinging broad shoulders, the muscular thighs. He also likes walking. We have such a lot in common, she thought, and then banished the thought. She was here to enjoy herself.

He stopped. They were perched halfway up the valley wall, its slopes rising and falling steeply. Here and there were little outcrops of white limestone. Apart from the two of them the place was still deserted.

'According to the man I talked to, these outcrops are made up of fossils,' he said. 'We'll collect a few for Holly then go for a further walk.'

'Sounds a good idea.' They scrambled up to the nearest outcrop. There they found the fossils, the bodies of tiny marine creatures from aeons ago. Lisa watched indulgently as Alex hammered and searched, looking for the most perfect specimens.

'What did you collect as a boy?' she asked.

He looked up, puzzled. 'I was a bird spotter. How did you know I collected anything?'

She grinned and pointed at the selection he had laid out neatly on the grass. 'Say I just guessed.'

It was fun, searching and sorting. 'We don't want to take too many,' he said. 'Leave some for other people.'

'You'd have a job to take too many. Look, are these trilobites?'

She leaned forward to pull at the stone. Her foot slipped on the uneven surface of the grass and she fell backwards. Alex was next to her and tried to save her. The two of them tottered and fell to the ground. Her ankle twisted, the breath slammed out of her body and a sudden, unbearable pain lanced through her back. She screamed. Alex was a dark shadow outlined against the blue sky above her. Shadow and sky dimmed into an all-encompassing greyness.

She didn't really faint. For a while she lay there, trying to cope with the pain—trying to understand why her life so suddenly had turned from happiness to this agony. She'd seen patients in Casualty doing the same, not believing that this pain was theirs.

Slowly she remembered where she was. Her eyes were shut, but there was the distinctive rocky smell that all walkers' clothes acquired. And there was another smell—the lemony tang of Alex's aftershave.

'Lisa, are you all right?'

There was more than anxiety in his voice, she thought. He sounded as if he... She couldn't decide how he sounded. 'My back. I think I fell on a rock.'

'Dear God.' There was one moment of horror in his voice, and then the doctor took over. 'Don't try to move. Can you feel your toes? Go on, wriggle them.'

She did. 'Yes, I can feel my toes and all my legs. There's no paralysis.'

'No tingling feeling in your hands, no difficulty breathing?'

'I can tell you've worked in Casualty, too. No, there's nothing seriously wrong.'

She opened her eyes to see him crouched over her. His anguished expression showed how upset he was—how much he cared for her?

'I'll decide if there's anything seriously wrong. Is it here that it hurts most? There's a spike of rock just by your side.' He pressed gently.

'Ow!' she said. 'Yes, that's it.'

'I think it could have been worse. Now, let me ease you onto your side, I want a closer look.'

It hurt to roll over, but she was happy to let him unzip her anorak, and ease aside her sweater and shirt. His hands were warm as he gently felt her side and ribs. 'I'm sorry,' he said as she dragged in a hissing breath, 'but...I don't think there are any ribs broken. Now I'm going to ease you up. Stop me if it hurts.'

It *did* hurt—but not seriously, she thought. He sat by her side, his arm around her. She glanced downwards at the spike of rock she'd fallen on, and shivered. Six inches to one side and she would have broken her back.

'A Casualty basic rule,' he said. 'Injuries seldom come singly. Have you any other pains?'

The question surprised her, but all her attention had been on the agony in her side. Were there any other pains? To her dismay, there were. 'I twisted my left ankle,' she said. 'I think it's sprained.'

'Well, we can't take your boot off to look or we'd never get it on again. We'll just have to rest it a while.'

He took her pulse.

'Testing for shock?' she asked professionally.

'Quite so. It's a bit low in volume but I don't think it's too bad. And you're showing no cyanosis or pallor. We'll rest here for a few minutes and then decide if we need to send for an ambulance.'

'No,' she said. 'I've seen enough people arriving in Casualty by ambulance who could easily have walked. I'll not turn out an ambulance.'

'Now how did I know that that would be your attitude?' he murmured. 'Anyway, we won't try to move yet.'

He zipped up her anorak and pulled the hood over her head. From his pocket he took a silver space blanket and wrapped it round her shoulders. Then he put his arm around her and gently pulled her to him.

It was only just in time. Suddenly she felt limp, frightened, near to tears. She pressed closer to Alex, and he took her pulse again.

'Thought so,' he muttered. 'Don't worry, darling, everything will be all right. The pain will go and we'll get you to a warm bed.'

She knew what he was doing. After an accident patients often went into shock. The best treatment was to keep them warm, reassure them and not move them. That was all Alex was doing for her. But, in spite of her pain, she was enjoying it. He was now the calm, competent doctor. But she remembered that moment when she'd first fallen. Perhaps he did have some regard for her.

For fifteen minutes they sat there together, her head on his chest and his arm around her. It was warm and comfortable. She'd have liked to have stayed there for ever. Her side and her ankle still throbbed with pain, but slowly the feeling of helplessness ebbed. She was not near to tears any more.

'I'd like to go now,' she said. 'I'm feeling a lot better.'

Alex took her pulse again, looked searchingly at her face, then kissed her briefly on the lips.

'OK, we'll move,' he said. 'But any problem and we stop.' He put his hands under her arms and lifted her effortlessly to her feet.

'Pick up the fossils,' she said. 'It would be silly to leave them now.'

He looked at her curiously, but did as she suggested. Then they moved back down to the path.

Walking wasn't too bad. Lisa favoured her bad ankle, and Alex took much of her weight. There wasn't the same cheery banter as before, but they made progress. Twice he made her stop to rest—she was glad he did. But eventually they reached the car.

He reclined the passenger seat and made her lie on it. From the boot he took a first-aid kit and had another look at her injured side. She could feel him dressing the cut, his fingers expert.

'I think the greatest pain will come from the abrasion and bruising,' he said. 'There's no need for stitching. Now, let's have a look at your foot.'

He took off her boot, and she leaned forward to look at her discoloured ankle. There was movement in it so it was only a sprain. He dipped a bandage in a nearby stream and bound the foot tightly. Then he gave her a couple of painkillers. She was glad as the pain was coming on again. They set off, with her still lying on the reclining seat. She began to feel giddy, disorientated.

After ten minutes Alex stopped in a layby, and fetched two cups of tea from a stall. Lisa pulled a face at hers—it was liberally spiked with sugar.

'This is horrible,' she said. 'I hate sweet tea.'

'Your blood sugar's down. This is medicine, not

pleasure. You know it's the right treatment.' She drank it.

They set off again. The car's movement was smooth, the faint hum of the motor lulled her and in five minutes she was asleep.

Waking up was less fun. 'Where are we?' she asked, trying to work out what the bright lights were.

'We're at Blazes' Casualty Department. It's not something I would usually do, but I'm going to try to jump the queue. I'll go inside and see who I can find.'

'No, Alex, I don't— Ooh!' It had been foolish to try to sit upright so quickly, but she recovered. 'You're a doctor, and you've looked after me.'

He looked down at her, an odd expression on his face. 'I don't want us to be doctor and patient any more. I want us to be man and woman.'

'Or friend and friend,' she said. 'All right, see if Mike Gee is in. He'll send me on my way.'

Mike *was* in, and he found time for her at once. Nothing was broken. Her ribs and ankle were strapped up, he gave her more painkillers and suggested she took time off work. She snorted. Then Alex helped her to limp out of the hospital.

'I'm sorry I spoiled your walk,' she said. 'Could you take me home and—?'

'D'you know what time it is?'

She hadn't thought of the time, and was amazed to find it only six o'clock.

'After our walk I had intended to take you to dinner in a pub somewhere,' he said. 'But now we're back I'll cook for you myself. You'd like that, wouldn't you?'

'Yes,' she said faintly, 'I think I would.'

CHAPTER FIVE

TOGETHER they walked to the front door of Alex's house. The pains in Lisa's side and ankle were now little more than distant aches. Something new was happening. She didn't think about what she was doing—her actions seemed to be pre-destined.

'Would you like to have a bath?' he asked her. 'Put a mild antiseptic in the water and when you've finished I'll put fresh dressings on.'

'Are you going to tell me to leave the bathroom door open?'

'Certainly,' he said sardonically, 'but I have no intention of coming in unless invited. Are you hungry?'

He took her hand and led her through to the kitchen. 'I'm ravenous, and this is something I can arrange.' In a side room were two great freezer cabinets. 'Lucy never prepares a single meal. She always cooks at least double quantity and freezes half.'

Lisa blinked at this efficiency. There was even a dated list of food available. 'I can cook,' she said. 'We don't need to raid your stores.'

Gently he said, 'You've done plenty today already. And I was going to take you out to dinner if you'd have let me. Now, what shall we have?'

Between them they settled on smoked haddock chowder, salmon and broccoli quiche and cheese from the larder. Then Alex went to his wine cupboard and fetched two bottles. He uncorked a red and put a white in the fridge.

'We're not going to drink two bottles?' she asked.

'Whatever's left can be recorked.' Then he took her to the bathroom upstairs and pointed to the cupboard where the towels were kept. It was an old-fashioned bathroom with plenty of space. As the bath filled she carefully took off her clothes. She shut the door—but didn't bolt it. Then she painfully climbed into the bath. It was good!

After twenty minutes there was a knock on the door. She grabbed the flannel, then wondered where to put it. Alex's voice called, 'Thought you might have difficulty putting on your climbing gear again. There's something outside you might like to borrow.' She put down the flannel with a sigh.

The heat had made her feel better. She climbed out of the bath and realised she was famished—it had been a long day. After putting on her underwear, she peered round the bathroom door to see a dark blue tracksuit. It was one of his, far too big for her but easy to get into and very comfortable. She put it on, arranged her clothes in a neat pile and carefully hob- bled downstairs.

He didn't hear her coming. When she opened the living-room door he was standing with his back to her, stripped to the waist. She'd never before realised how sensual a man's back could be. He had the firm body of an athlete, the long indentation of his spine buttressed by the great *erector spinae* muscles. The wing-shaped *latissimus dorsi* swept from his waist to under his arms, flexing as he moved. At the base of his spine was the faintest patch of blonde hair. She had seen it before on babies.

His skin was smooth and white—but just over his

hip was a great bruise, with blood congealed round a split in its centre. 'How did you do that?' she gasped.

He turned, smiling ruefully. 'I think I bounced on the same rock as you did. We were very close—remember?'

'But you said nothing! You looked after me and you must have been in agony!'

He shrugged. 'Certainly it hurt, but nothing like as badly as yours did.'

'Let me see. I'll do that.' He had a first-aid box by him, and was trying to dab the wound with disinfectant-soaked cotton wool.

'It is a bit hard to get at,' he admitted.

She cleaned the wound, marvelling again that he had said nothing. Then she strapped on a dressing.

'My turn to see to you now,' he said, and she pulled up her tracksuit top so he could re-dress her injury. Then he bandaged her ankle again.

'I suppose you're my patient now,' he said, 'but, there again, I'm also your patient.' Quickly he bent and kissed her. 'Now are we both guilty of professional misconduct?'

Her heart was hammering. 'I'm hungry,' she said. 'Let's forget about being professional.'

Both were aware of the smells coming from the warming drawer of the oven. He led her into the kitchen. He had set two places side by side on the table, and proceeded to put all the food onto a central warming plate.

'Now we don't have to jump up and down,' he said. 'We can sit, eat, drink and be happy.'

'Sounds good.'

He uncorked the white wine from the fridge, poured them a glass each and asked her to taste. First she was aware of coolness, then there was an explosion of tastes on her palate. She could taste fruit, the silkiness of elderberry, she thought, and something almost metallic afterwards. When she swallowed the taste lingered. It was glorious! She looked at him. 'I see the supermarket was having an offer,' she said.

For a moment he looked shocked before he realised she was teasing him. 'I like people who taste wine,' he said. 'You don't need to know all about grapes and vineyards. Just enjoy what it does for you.'

She sipped again. If anything, it was better than before.

She hadn't realised how hungry she was. Because of the barbecue she knew Lucy was a good cook, but this meal was tremendous. 'It's been a long day,' he said, watching approvingly as she ate. 'How d'you think I'd manage as a casualty nurse?'

She sniffed. 'On a busy Saturday I would have dealt with a dozen like me in the first half of the evening. As well as the serious cases, that is. You did remember to bring in the fossils?'

'Yes. I shan't tell Holly the pain they cost you.'

'Why? Would she worry?'

'A little, perhaps. But she'd have to tell the teacher the full story, and expect special consideration because she'd suffered by proxy.'

They both laughed. She knew this was an evening she wouldn't forget. Because they were both hurt she could pretend she didn't feel threatened by him. Or by herself. So she gave herself to food, drink and conversation.

Alex told her about his summers in Gloucestershire as a boy, his first hopes of being a doctor and the desperate months of preparing for A levels, hoping to get high enough grades. That was a feeling she remembered herself.

She told him things about herself which, perhaps, no one else knew—how she cried into her pillow for her mother, first after she'd left and then after she'd died.

'I loved my two sisters dearly, but at times I resented the demands they made on me. And then I felt ashamed for the resentment.'

'It's understandable,' he said. 'But I'll bet they love you now.'

With the chowder and quiche they drank white wine, then with the cheese he brought out the bottle of red. It had a totally different taste, rich and oaky. The perfect companion for the creaminess of the Stilton.

'That was a wonderful meal,' she said finally, dabbing up the last few crumbs of cheese with a wetted fingertip. 'If you eat like this all the time I'm surprised you aren't fatter.'

'Ah. Lucy keeps a tight rein on me. She says the better the food the less of it you need. She— Ow!'

He had tried to stand and she saw the twinge of pain mirrored in his eyes. 'You didn't have a bath, like me, so you're getting stiff,' she said in a matter-of-fact tone. 'It's to be expected. Come on, sit on the couch and then I'll fetch the coffee.'

'I'm not the invalid—you are,' he said mock-seriously. 'I'll fetch the coffee.'

She shook her head. 'I love men when they're in pain and trying to be macho, but you've done everything so far and movement will be good for me.'

They moved through the hall to the leather couch in the living room. He threw a match into the previously set fire. Then, just before lowering himself onto the couch, he kissed her—again.

It was a soft, sweet kiss. There was nothing threatening about it, his hands on her shoulders and his lips barely brushing hers. 'You're good to me, Lisa,' he said.

The world spun around her, but from somewhere she summoned the strength to reply. Lightly she said, 'I can see you're feeling better. Sit here and I'll fetch the coffee.' She fled into the kitchen.

He had prepared everything—cups, biscuits, primed the espresso machine. But as she mechanically went about her tasks she knew that things had changed.

Kissing her once could be seen as a gesture of friendship. But by kissing her a second time he had brought crashing down the structure of deceit she had hidden behind. When she went back into the room she would be—unprotected. Not from him but from herself. For a moment she thought seriously about walking out, calling a taxi. Then there was a rasping hiss from the machine, and she carefully poured out the coffee.

He had moved to the side of the couch, to where he could reach the music centre. As she walked into the room she was met by the soft strains of the beginning of Ravel's 'Bolero'. How did he know how much she loved that piece of music? The same short but intense tune, repeated time after time, gaining volume and passion and finally crashing into a frenzied climax.

'Do you like this?' he asked as she placed the coffee in front of him.

'It's one of my favourite pieces,' she told him. 'It's so...exciting.'

'I don't know much about your taste in music. I'd like to. In fact, there's a lot of things I'd like to know about you.'

She tried to be brisk, to ignore his plea to know her better. 'I like music with a tune and a beat. I like some Beethoven and most of the Beatles. And I like dance music.'

'Good. Our tastes are similar.' He watched her take her coffee and retire to the safety of a chair on the other side of the low table in front of the couch.

'That's not very friendly, is it?' he asked, his voice mild. 'You're not afraid of me, are you? Come and sit by me.'

Yes, she was afraid—but not of him. Still, she came and sat next to him. It was a very comfortable couch, high-backed with soft cushions. She could sink into it. Together they drank coffee in companionable silence. She stared into the fire, the flames sputtering and the logs crackling as it took hold. 'We had a fire like that at home,' she said. 'The family used to sit and watch it in the dark.'

In the background was the insistent beat of the 'Bolero'.

Both leaned forward at the same time to put their cups down. As they leaned back she slid nearer to him, and he put his arm round her shoulders. For a while they just sat there, and then she leaned closer, leaned her head on his shoulder and put her free arm round him. Where she was going she didn't know. It seemed that for once decisions were being made for her.

She could feel the warmth of his breath, and distantly under her arm was the beating of his heart. When he turned to kiss her it seemed the most natural thing in the world. His touch was hesitant, his lips merely caressing hers. He kissed her face, brushing her cheeks, her closed eyes, the sensitive lobes of her ears.

It all felt so good, so natural. As his grip tightened on her she found herself sliding her arms under the loose tracksuit top to stroke the firm-ridged abdomen, the muscles of his chest. He sighed and gasped as her questing fingers grazed his nipples, and his mouth burned down on hers.

There was nothing she could do to stop herself, nothing she wanted to do. She was swept away on a rip tide of feeling like nothing she had ever experienced before. She pulled him to her as her mouth opened under his insidious pressure, drinking in his sweetness as she'd done with no other man.

'Lisa,' he whispered hoarsely, 'my Lisa.' And still she could hear the 'Bolero' inexorably moving to its climax.

There seemed to be no fumbling, no embarrassed wrestling with clothes or underwear, but suddenly her tracksuit top was gone, her bra undone. Alex leaned back so he could hold and stroke her, and she saw his eyes darken with passion. In his hands her breasts felt heavy, the twin peaks erect as a sign of her own longing. His head bowed and swooped as he tenderly took each in turn in his mouth. Her head stretched back with the ecstasy of it.

Slowly they leaned so she was stretched along the broad couch, and he pulled at her tracksuit bottoms. Willingly she helped him slide them down, throwing the garment away so she was naked to him but for the tiniest pair of white briefs. She knew nothing but the rightness of what she was doing, the pleasure he was giving her, the pleasure she could give him. He was so gentle. He took such care of her injured body.

Now he, too, had shrugged off the top of his tracksuit and their half-naked bodies were pressed together. She could feel the heat of his skin, smell his maleness. With one hand she cupped his neck, pulled his head even closer to her. Her arm slid further round his waist to hug him—

It broke through his passion. There was the sudden hissing intake of breath, the jerk of a body in pain. She had—with all her strength she had squeezed his injured ribs. He must be in agony! Instantly she released him.

'It doesn't matter,' he muttered. 'Just be with me and…'

But it did matter. She reached forward and ran her hand over his forehead. The dampness there was from pain not passion. 'I'm sorry, I'm sorry,' she cried. 'What did I do to you?'

'It doesn't matter,' he gasped. 'Lisa, come back, let me hold you. It doesn't matter.'

But, of course, it mattered. She was a nurse, she didn't cause people pain. More than that, she was about to make love to him. Did she want to? She slid back along the couch.

She looked down at herself, practically naked. Then she looked at Alex, a curl of hair drooping over his damp forehead and in his eyes an expression of sadness. He knew. Even at that moment she could marvel at his sensitivity. She knew he wouldn't try to touch her unless she made the first move.

In the suddenly heightened silence the last few bars of the 'Bolero' blasted out their discordant climax. Nice sense of timing, she thought bitterly.

She looked at her nakedness again. 'I...I'd like to get dressed,' she said tremulously.

The silence between them stretched on interminably. 'All right,' he said. 'Perhaps you should. But please—just wait one minute. For one minute I want to look at you. To remember?'

'Just one minute, then.' She looked at his stricken face, passion warring with sadness. For a full minute she waited, and then she reached for her clothes.

Lisa knew he was entitled to some kind of explanation, and she desperately wanted him to understand. 'I didn't lead you on deliberately,' she said, as she fumbled with the zip. 'I'm sorry if you think that I—'

'I don't blame you, Lisa.' Alex's voice was hoarse, but she could feel the kindness. It made her feel worse.

'I'm a virgin,' she went on, 'but that's not what stopped me. I...I feel a lot for you.' She knew she mustn't use the word 'love', but despairingly she knew that it was the right one. 'I just can't sleep with you unless I think that...that... Well, I only want to sleep with the man I'm going to marry.' There, she'd said it. 'I'm sorry, I'm so sorry.'

She was dressed now, and he reached over and kissed her on the cheek. 'I'm sorry, too,' he said. 'It was something I started and I shouldn't have. I hope you'll forgive me.'

'There's nothing to forgive. I wanted you as much as you wanted me.'

It was strange. Passion had now gone and she was left with a lethargy just as if their affair had come to a consummation. But her feeling for him was as strong.

'Do you want to go? Shall I run you home?' His

voice was sympathetic, not cruel. He was still her
friend. But she didn't want to go yet. She had been
strong but she was entitled to something.

'I don't want to go yet if you'll let me stay a bit
longer. You must be tired. Why don't you lie out on
the couch. I'll lie by your side, but that must be all.'

'If you wish, that will be all. Lisa—'

'No more talking,' she said.

She would have thought it impossible, but his blue
eyes closed and after a while she could tell that he
slept. She laid her head on his shoulder and she, too,
slept, a strange half-sleep which she protected jeal-
ously from waking. This would have to be the last
time. Then consciousness slipped from her as well.

At twenty to twelve she woke by his side. The tick-
ing of the antique clock on the mantelpiece seemed
very loud. The fire had burned down to red ash. She
told herself that she had a curfew. She had fifteen
minutes of joy left and then, like Cinderella, she was
back to cinders and misery. She seemed to be thinking
about Cinderella a lot these days. But at least
Cinderella didn't have to see Prince Charming every
day.

She thought about how happy she'd been for a
while, how suited she and Alex were, how she'd had,
for the shortest time, the promise of ecstasy. Now it
was gone.

The minutes ticked by inexorably. At five minutes
before midnight her self-imposed time was up so—
the hardest thing she'd ever done in her life—she got
up. She edged away from him carefully and went upstairs to put her clothes in a bag.

Just as she pulled on her boots she knew he was

awake. Turning, she saw his blue eyes fastened on her.

'How's the side?' she asked briskly, trying to be a nurse.

He dismissed the question with the contempt it deserved. 'My back's not important. You're the one who is hurt. How are you?'

'I'm stiff but there's no great pain now.'

'I didn't mean your injuries. Do you have to go?'

'Yes, I'll call for a taxi. You'd better take a couple of painkillers and go to bed.' Giving simple, prosaic instructions calmed her.

'You could stay. There's a spare room, I promise that—'

She interrupted him. 'We both made a mistake. Fortunately, we stopped before it was too late. Alex, you know I...I have a high regard for you.' The pompous words sounded ludicrous. She was aware that both of them knew what she meant, but she couldn't say it. 'But I've got to have a regard for myself.'

He sat up, and the sight of the naked chest where she had lain five minutes before was almost more than she could bear. 'I can understand that,' he said desolately, 'and I can respect it.'

'Then you know why I must go?'

He nodded. 'You must make your decisions, Lisa. But you won't phone for a taxi. I'll drive you home now.'

'Thank you,' she whispered.

Rosalind was waiting for her when she got home. As ever, her books were spread out neatly, her glass of milk in its place. A fresh terror gripped Lisa. 'There's nothing new about Dad?' she asked.

'Nothing. We won't hear for a week or so. There's a big party on in the residence but I don't fancy the riotous life just now. You don't mind if I stay overnight?'

Lisa smiled. The more Rosalind avoided the hectic residence social life the more she was invited out. Still, it was good that she was here. Lisa needed to be with someone who was non-threatening, who shared the same values as her. She also had an almost unbearable need of uncomplicated companionship. 'I'll do us some supper,' she said.

Rosalind looked up. 'That tracksuit belongs to someone else,' she said, 'and you're limping and moving as if you're in pain.' She stared more closely at Lisa's face. 'Something is wrong. Tell me, big sister.'

Lisa couldn't speak. She stood, looking at the small silver-eyed figure of her sister. Rosalind had the self-contained confidence of a cat.

'Sit down,' Rosalind commanded, 'and I'll make supper. Then you can tell me.'

She made the traditional cocoa and toast then sat, waiting until Lisa was ready to talk.

'I've had a bit of an accident,' Lisa said. 'Look, I've sprained my ankle and hurt my side.'

Rosalind examined her injuries. 'Nasty, but not enough to make you look like you do. What else happened?'

Lisa didn't know how or where to start. 'It was a very good talk in Leeds,' she said wildly. 'I'll get you a photocopy of the notes they gave me.'

Rosalind's eyes gleamed. 'I'd like that. Now keep talking.'

Perhaps telling Rosalind would get her own confused thoughts in order. Trying to be casual, Lisa talked about the walk in Derbyshire, her fall, the dinner she'd had afterwards. Just as it might have happened.

'What's he like, this Dr Scott?'

'Oh, he's good. We all like him. He's got time for everybody, never is harassed or loses his temper. He's a very good clinician too. I've learned a lot from him.'

Rosalind said flatly, 'You're not telling me something. What are you hiding?'

Lisa winced. Her other sister didn't have this icy skill in analysis but somehow Rosalind seemed to ferret out everything.

'I nearly slept with him,' she said. 'Rosalind, I think I've fallen for him quite badly.'

'Really in love?' Rosalind asked. 'I know you've had boyfriends before, but none of them made much impression. Is this real love?'

'I think so. It must be, it hurts enough.'

Rosalind was remorseless. 'So, what's the problem? Doesn't he love you?'

'Well, yes… I think he likes me a lot. But he's been married already and says it's a mistake he won't make again. He's made it quite clear he's not interested in anything but a casual affair.'

'And I know you won't have that.'

'No,' said Lisa, 'I will not.'

'Then you're just going to have to forget him. There are other men.'

This was just what Lisa didn't want to hear. 'I might have guessed you'd say something like that,' she groaned. 'Have you no feelings at all? One day you'll be in love then you'll know what rubbish you're talking!'

'I'm not talking rubbish about this man,' said Rosalind. 'I'm talking cruel good sense. Oh, Lisa, what are you going to do?'

Lisa fell sobbing onto her shoulder.

CHAPTER SIX

FORTUNATELY the pain from ankle and side had largely passed by Monday morning. It was a good thing because Lisa needed to work, and life on the ward was quite hard.

There was good news. Mr Ralston, their sleeping sickness patient, was making a recovery and had been discharged. But there was also bad news. Sir Arthur had admitted two new patients. 'I don't know that there's an awful lot can be done for either of them, Lisa,' he said, shaking his head dolefully, 'but I'm sure they will get devoted nursing.'

He opened the case notes. 'Mr Kewing here. Not an uncommon story, I'm afraid. He lives alone, keeps to himself. Proud of the fact that he hadn't been to the doctor for fifteen years. Eventually he did go to his GP, complaining of breathlessness and blood-stained sputum. The GP sent him to me, and here are his X-rays.'

Lisa looked at the 'salt and pepper' appearance of the pictures and winced. 'Pulmonary tuberculosis?'

'We could have treated it if we'd had him in sooner. As it is, the infection has spread to the brain. He also has tuberculous meningitis.' She knew what the treatment would be—a cocktail of antibiotics such as ethambutol and rifampicin, with the old favourite, streptomycin, kept in reserve.

'What's his general condition like?' she asked.

'As you might guess, poor. His temperature is very

high. We've got an IV line in, trying to pump some nourishment into him, and all we can do otherwise is hope.'

Hope wasn't enough for Mr Kewing. He lapsed into coma, and two days later died peacefully. There was an attempt at establishing his contacts, but no one could find out where he had contracted the disease. He might have been infected for years.

No one came to visit Mr Kewing. He had lived in a rented house and had no friends, no relations. His next of kin appeared to be a married sister in Australia, who sent him regular Christmas cards.

As Lisa filled in the necessary paperwork she was filled with a great sense of depression. She had family, friends, but not a husband or children of her own. Could she end up like Mr Kewing? She told herself she was being morbid, and set about something else.

The second case was just the opposite.

'I've admitted a Mrs Pearson,' said Sir Arthur. He sounded, unusually for him, a little harassed. 'Er—could you have a word with the family?'

'Certainly,' Lisa said, surprised that Sir Arthur felt he needed to ask.

'They're very—supportive,' said Sir Arthur.

She realised what he meant when she saw them.

Ada Pearson was 'Our Gran'. Within three miles of her council flat lived four sons and three daughters. There was a bewildering number of grandchildren and quite a handful of great-grandchildren. Lisa never quite worked out which was which.

Our Gran was vast. She ate without stopping and never took exercise—in fact, she never did anything. Now she was quite seriously ill with influenza. In spite of being one of those at high risk, she hadn't felt like having an anti-flu vaccination. At first the family had ignored her complaints about pains behind the breastbone and aching muscles—apparently, these were common occurrences with Our Gran. Only when she'd collapsed had the family eventually called the doctor, who'd realised that for once her condition was serious.

Sir Arthur prescribed bedrest, with antiviral drugs and antibiotics as well, knowing there was a chance of a chest infection. But both he and Lisa knew that the prognosis was not good for a woman so large with a heart condition. 'A particularly nasty virus,' Sir Arthur grumbled. 'I hope it doesn't spread too far.'

The hospital tried to operate an open ward system, and for three days Lisa coped with a constant procession of visitors. Just for once she found herself longing for the time when hospitals had insisted on no more than two per bedside and strict visiting times.

Ada's room filled with get-well cards—many hand-drawn. There were flowers and fruit and chocolates. Eventually Lisa had to say that there were too many visitors—they were overtiring the patient. Could the visitors limit themselves? But the Pearson family was not good at organisation. She had to tell every single visitor.

And through it all was Ada, slowly getting worse. It took Sir Arthur and Lisa most of a day to explain that Our Gran was seriously ill, they might have to expect the worst and, no, there was nothing more to do that had not already been done.

Ada died late one night, as everyone on the ward knew she would. Paradoxically, Lisa found herself missing the great tribe of the Pearson family—the wives smoking guiltily out of the window, the children running up and down the ward, the loud arguments echoing round Ada's bed, in which Ada had never taken part.

Sir Arthur and Lisa were invited to the funeral. She managed to take an hour off and slip into the back of the church for the service.

Alex had been good with the Pearson clan. He'd been able to manage them better than Sir Arthur. He'd remained imperturbable, courteous, happy to explain to even the youngest child just what was wrong with our Gran.

'You're an hour late, leaving the ward,' Lisa had pointed out to him one day, 'just because of the Pearsons.'

'I don't mind. I was early leaving poor Mr Kewing. There was no one to talk to about him, and I wished there were.'

Lisa had nodded.

She'd managed a brief private talk with Alex the first time he'd come onto the ward. She knew something had to be said.

First, though, she could act as a nurse. 'How's the side?' she asked professionally.

'The pain's completely gone. More to the point, how d'you feel?'

'A lot better. I think having instant care helped.'

'Yes.' He paused. 'Lisa, there are other things we should talk about. Perhaps we could—'

She interrupted him. 'Alex, we have to work together. You know how I feel, about you and about what nearly happened. I'm asking you to help me. We can stay friends, but I shouldn't see as much of you as I have been doing.'

'Are you sure that's what you want?' he asked intensely. 'There's nothing I can say to make you change your mind?'

'Nothing you can say. You will help me, won't you?'

'Of course, I will,' he said sadly. 'But do you know what it's costing me? Do you know what I feel every time I see you? I'm nearly out of my mind!'

'Alex, for now I'm going to be selfish. I've got my own feelings to deal with.' She paused. 'You're going to ask why we can't have our own little bit of happiness, say that what we do together won't hurt anyone. It'd be our secret. I've had offers like this before, Alex, and it's just not for me. Especially since I care for you so much. So, you will help me?'

'Of course I will. But it's hard.'

There was another thing she had to say, and it was difficult. 'I don't want you to think that I'm trying to, well, trap you into something you don't want.'

He smiled. 'You sweet, old-fashioned thing. No, you know I don't think that. I think too much of you.'

And he had stood by his word. He didn't spend more time in her room than was necessary, politely declining her offers of coffee. But she knew from the odd glance that he was suffering, and she knew she was suffering too.

'You know, I think there's nothing worse than messing around with a man you feel you daren't touch,' Sarah said to her one day as they were checking the drugs wagon. 'Nothing more soul-destroying.'

'I'm sure you're right,' Lisa said, trying to be careless in her answer, 'but what brought on this great thought?'

'What you and Alex are doing to each other is painful to watch,' Sarah said.

Lisa was stricken. 'Is it that obvious?' she burst out. She'd tried so hard to be discreet, to be casual in their relationship. The very last thing she needed right now was hospital gossip.

'Only to me,' Sarah said, 'but, then, I'm an expert. Cheer up and fight it, Sister. The first two years are the worst.'

'Two years? Yes, I can see it taking two years. And they'll be hard.'

'You're not tempted, then?' Sarah asked. 'You don't feel like saying to hell with it—why can't I grab what I want?'

'I'm tempted all right,' Lisa said gloomily. 'Oh, how I'm tempted. I feel I'm out of step with everyone else, but basically I'm a conventional girl.'

'Stick to your guns,' Sarah advised. 'You'll be happier in the long run.'

To Lisa, it just seemed a very long run.

Brian Barnes had now started to visit Marie in the evenings when Lisa wasn't on duty. She'd warned the night and evening staff, but evening visiting was always busy and there was a limit to what could be done.

'I'm sure he's bringing her something in,' Alex said to Lisa, on one of the infrequent occasions they spoke. 'See what you can get out of her, will you, Lisa?'

Lisa promised to try, but she knew it would be difficult. Sometimes Marie would be chatty, telling Lisa horrifying stories about her life and the people she mixed with. Gently Lisa tried to encourage her to see that there was hope, that if she visited the drug dependency unit she could be cured.

'Drug addiction is a disease, Marie, just like hepatitis or tuberculosis. You *can* be cured. It's painful but it's possible. You've just got to want to be cured.'

'Brian would never let me,' was the dull reply.

Lisa hesitated, knowing she was on dangerous ground. 'Do you have to stay with Brian?' she asked.

'He'd never let me go. Besides, who else have I got? Nobody.'

At other times Marie would be awkward and unpleasant, telling Lisa she was an interfering old witch and to leave her alone. Lisa felt even more sorry for her then. She knew what was happening. Marie's body craved drugs and the methadone they gave her every morning wasn't enough to satisfy it.

Eventually Alex and Lisa had had enough. Alex was sent for late one night after Barnes had visited. Merely by listening to Marie's breathing and looking at her pinpoint pupils, he could tell what had happened. She'd had more drugs. Lisa now agreed. Whatever effect it had on Marie, Barnes had to be stopped from visiting her.

Unusually, Barnes came in the afternoon the next day and Lisa bleeped for Alex. He was on the ward within minutes and spoke directly to Barnes.

'I have a security officer outside. If you visit this ward again you will be taken downstairs, searched for drugs and the police informed. Now get out and don't come back.'

Barnes tried to put up a fight. 'You can't talk to me like that. This is a public hospital. I can come in when I want.'

'Can you? Yesterday you gave a controlled substance to one of my patients. I have blood samples that will prove she ingested it, and only you visited her. If you don't get off this ward now I shall phone the police.'

'I'll take her out of here!'

'She can sign herself out, but if she does I guarantee she'll die.'

Barnes backed off a little. 'If she dies it'll be the hospital's fault. She's an addict—she needs more than you give her.'

'I thought I told you to go.'

Barnes left. Alex shook his head as he watched the man, stabbing furiously at the lift button, and said, 'I usually think of myself as a bit of a liberal, I try to look for the good in people, but if I could execute large-scale drug peddlers I think I'd be quite happy.'

'You mean that, don't you?' Lisa asked curiously. 'You're a doctor, dedicated to saving life, yet you'd condemn some people to death.'

'A few people. No one should be able to cause such large-scale misery.'

'Do you include Barnes?'

Alex shook his head. 'He's a miserable, evil little so-and-so, but he's a victim, too. I'm talking about people who sell drugs but never take them.'

There didn't seem anything further for the two of them to say, but Lisa was loath to part from him. Just being next to him was pleasing, giving her a momentary feeling of warmth. And it was only for a minute. He seemed to feel the same way.

'Thanks for calling me,' he said after a while. 'Is everything...else all right?'

Lisa understood his question but elected not to answer it. 'Now Barnes has gone the ward is quiet,' she assured him. 'No need to worry about anything.'

'No need to worry about anything,' he echoed. 'I'm

glad to hear it, Sister—even if I don't entirely believe it.' Then he was gone, striding so swiftly down the ward that he almost seemed to be running.

Three days later Lisa stopped her little Fiesta at some lights a few hundred yards from Alex's home. She was about to accelerate away when she saw Lucy, holding the hands of Holly and Jack. She would have liked to have driven past but Holly saw her and waved frantically so Lisa stopped and reversed so they could talk. She climbed out of the car.

'We haven't seen you for a while,' Holly said reproachfully. 'I wanted to say thank you for those fossils you got with Daddy. I've learned all the words like "crinoids" and "trilobites". My teacher's ever so pleased and Daddy's promised me we can all go and get some more. Why haven't you been to see us?'

Lisa realised she'd missed the two children—and their grandmother, too, who was looking at her with a speculative eye. Feeling guilty, she said, 'Work's been quite hectic recently. I just haven't had time.'

The children accepted this. Lisa felt that Lucy didn't. 'Would you all like a lift home?' she asked.

The children chorused, 'Yes, please.' When Lucy nodded, they climbed energetically into the back seat. Lisa looked at Lucy, a little concerned. She seemed pale.

'I've been under the weather a bit,' she explained. 'Nothing to worry about.' Checking to make sure that Holly and Jack couldn't hear, she went on, 'I guess you and Alex had a bit of a spat over something. He hasn't been his usual sunny self recently.'

'He's been all right on the ward,' Lisa said. She didn't know what else to say. Lucy was too shrewd.

'I'll bet you've not seen as much of him as usual. Something is upsetting him. I'm his mother, I live with him and I know him.' She sighed. 'Still, I decided long ago not to interfere unless I'm asked. He must organise his own life. Lisa, if you'd like to come round to see us when he's not there we'd be ever so pleased to see you.'

After a moment's fraught silence, Lisa said, 'I don't want to do anything behind his back, but I would love to call.'

'Fair enough. He's going to America in a week or two so call then.'

Lisa felt hollow inside. Was he going to see his exwife?

'He's going to a conference,' Lucy put in quickly, 'in Seattle.'

She must have guessed what I was thinking, Lisa thought.

'Anyway, will you come to tea one day then?'

'I'd love to,' Lisa said sincerely, 'or you could all come to my flat, if you liked.'

'Perhaps we'll do both,' Lucy smiled, obviously cheered at the prospect. 'It'll be our little secret. Can you drop us off at home now? I'm feeling a bit cold.'

Lisa refused an invitation to call in at the house and drove home. She wasn't sure of her own feelings. She liked Lucy and the children, but being with them reminded her of Alex. It was a bitter-sweet relationship.

She saw more of Alex over the next few days. He explained that he was shortly going to Seattle to a conference on infectious diseases and techniques of dealing with penicillin-resistant bacteria so he was taking over some of Sir Arthur's work as Sir Arthur would cover for him in his absence.

'It sounds really interesting,' said Lisa, falsely bright.

'I'm sure it will be. A pity you couldn't come as well—it would be pleasant if we could go together.' She opened her mouth, then shut it again. She could only make things worse.

It happened a week later. A quietish Thursday afternoon, Alex was somewhere on the ward, discussing a problem with Paul Evans. Under Alex's guidance Paul was blossoming, turning into a caring and informed doctor. Lisa had noticed that he'd even adopted some of Alex's body language, such as the way Alex would lean over a patient and smile.

Her phone rang. It was Alex's office, rerouting a call to him. A man on the phone introduced himself as Dr Brangwen. Lisa recognised the name—she'd met him before. The man was a well-thought-of GP who had a practice close to her own home. He asked to speak to Dr Scott, as a matter of some urgency.

She fetched Alex and waited outside her room. A minute later he opened the door and called her in.

'Alex, are you all right?' she gasped.

He wasn't. His face was white, and there was a thin line of perspiration on his lip. When he spoke there was a tremor in the usually even tones, his West Country accent more pronounced.

'Nothing wrong with me. But there is with Lucy. Lisa, can you find Sir Arthur and ask him to come up here?'

'Of course. What's wrong?'

He made an obvious effort to speak normally. 'Now

I know what other people feel. That was our GP on the phone. Lucy called him out. She'd been suffering from a headache and had been violently sick. It's not like her to send for the doctor. When he got to see her he found she was avoiding the light and couldn't put her head between her knees. She had mild convulsions while he was there. He's sending her here by ambulance.'

She knew at once what Alex feared. 'You think she's got meningitis,' she said.

'It's a definite possibility. I'll go down to Casualty and get her sent here, if you can find Sir Arthur.'

'I'll get a bed ready as well,' she said, and, as he left, reached for the phone.

'Medical people are worst where relations are concerned,' Sir Arthur said calmly when she reached him. 'I'll go straight to Casualty myself. See you quite shortly, Sister.'

It wasn't long before the trolley was being wheeled along, Lucy's pinched white face making her seem older than she was. Lisa got Sarah to help her into bed. She knew that for some people it was better to be helped by a stranger than by someone they knew well.

'If you'll help me with my examination, Sister,' Sir Arthur said. 'Alex, you will, of course, stay here in the office. We'll talk in a moment, but she is my patient, not yours.'

'Of course,' Alex agreed.

Lisa had already prepared a trolley. She entered the little room with Sir Arthur and told Sarah to go and make Alex a strong coffee. 'Sorry to be a problem,' came a faint voice from the bed.

Lisa took Lucy's hand and stroked it, and Sir

Arthur said quietly, 'You're causing no problem, Mrs Scott. We just want to do a couple of tests.'

Lucy's neck was now very stiff. Sir Arthur frowned. Then he lifted Lucy's thigh until it was at right angles to her body, and gently tried to straighten her leg. Lucy gasped with the pain and Sir Arthur compressed his lips. This was Kernig's sign—usually an infallible indication of meningitis.

'I think we'll start with intravenous penicillin before we get the lab results,' Sir Arthur murmured to Lisa, 'and I need to do a lumbar puncture to examine the cerebrospinal fluid.'

Lisa nodded. This was the usual treatment. She knew it was vital to start the treatment for meningitis as quickly as possible. Lucy had been very lucky that her GP had spotted it so quickly.

She helped Lucy over onto her side, trying to comfort her for what she knew that many patients dreaded. 'Lumbar puncture,' Lucy whispered. 'No problem. Alex has done hundreds of them.'

Eventually the procedure was finished and Sir Arthur examined the fluid he had drawn off. It was purulent, not clear—a sign of meningococci or staphylococci as the infective agent. Sir Arthur pursed his lips and went to see Alex, leaving Lisa alone with Lucy. 'What about the children, Lisa?' Lucy whispered. 'They'll be home from school soon. Who'll look after them?'

'I will. Just rest and get better, Lucy. I'll see to them,' she volunteered before she had time to think.

She caught Alex just as he was about to enter the room. 'Your mother's worried about the children. I've told her I'll look after them for a day or two. If that's all right with you.'

He looked at her in wonderment. 'You'd do that for me?'

'No, I'd do it for them. I like them and Lucy. It's not too much to ask, is it?'

'I can phone our neighbour. She's bringing the kids home today, and will happily give them tea and look after them for the first half of this evening.'

'We'll talk later, then.' She went back to her office as he disappeared inside his mother's room. He was with her again ten minutes later.

'I'm pretty sure it is bacterial meningitis,' he said, 'although the lab will tell for certain. I agree with Sir Arthur's treatment and—'

She reached over and tugged at the arm of his white coat. 'Alex,' she said gently, 'I know you can't help worrying, but she's not your patient. You're her son not her doctor. You must act like a son.'

He looked down at her hand, still clutching his sleeve. For a moment he covered it with his own. 'I know,' he said. 'You're good to me, Lisa.'

For a second she was tempted to put her arms round him to comfort him. So far in their relationship he had always been the tough one. Now for once she saw him made vulnerable by love for his mother. But she daren't make any such move. It might prove how vulnerable she was.

'There are arrangements to be made,' she said practically. 'We have to think things through. You'll want to stay here near your mother. I'll pick up the kids, put them to bed, stay the night and get them off to school in the morning. I can arrange to arrive here a little later tomorrow. Just don't worry about them. I can cope.'

'I can't think of anyone I'd sooner have looking after them. You know how much in your debt I'll be?'

'Yes, I do. That's why I'm mentioning one thing more, Alex. We've had an understanding recently and it's…worked. More or less.' Her voice was cracking but she stumbled on. 'We carry on with the agreement. We're friends, nothing more.'

'I hope it doesn't cost you too much, Lisa,' he said bleakly. 'Believe me, I really do. Now, details…' There were keys, neighbours' phone numbers, details of the house alarm—a dozen things to sort out. But minutes later he went back to sit with his mother.

I wonder what I've done, Lisa asked herself.

First she drove home and packed herself an overnight bag. She didn't change out of her uniform. Then she left a message for Rosalind and drove to Alex's home. It felt strange, letting herself in with his key.

It wasn't exactly his house; he had rented it for a year while he took time to look for exactly what he wanted. But somehow bits of his personality were imprinted on it. She peered into the little room he used as a study. There was his computer on the desk and piles of books, some of them still unpacked. There were pictures of Lucy and the children on the walls.

She went to Lucy's room next to the children's, pulled the sheets off and remade it. A nurse again. Then the bell downstairs indicated that the friendly neighbour had brought back the children. Alex had phoned her, explaining what was happening.

The neighbour, Mrs Wragg, seemed to think that everything was quite proper, probably because Lisa was still in uniform. After asking about Lucy, she said she'd pick up the children tomorrow at half past eight and later on keep them for tea as well. She could manage that for quite a while—she knew Lucy would do the same for her. Lisa smiled. In her time she had done this swapping of kids and responsibilities when Emily and Rosalind had been young. She rather liked it.

It was fun, looking after Holly and Jack. They accepted Lucy's sudden illness with the carelessness that children have. Being looked after by Lisa was a definite adventure. They'd had their tea, but Holly wanted to help Lisa make hers.

Lisa scrambled eggs and tore up salad, showing Holly how to make a dressing out of oil and balsamic vinegar. 'And a little bit of this?' asked Jack, lifting a bottle from the shelf. Lisa looked at the chili powder and shook her head. When she sat down to eat she found she wasn't hungry so her eggs were thrown away.

They watched television, then Lisa bathed the children and read them a story. 'Daddy's working tonight but promises he'll come and see you,' she said.

When they were asleep she changed out of her uniform and went downstairs to read. It had been a long day and she was tired. But she was enjoying herself. She didn't ask herself why.

She jumped when the phone rang, but it was Rosalind. As ever, she listened without comment while Lisa explained what she was doing.

'All very good of you,' she said when Lisa had finished. 'But no more than I would expect. The trouble is, Lisa, that this man isn't a neighbour or a friend off the ward. He's someone you think you love and you're trying to get away from. Sharing a ward is bad enough. It's worse if you're sharing a house and kids.'

Lisa had thought exactly that herself but she wasn't going to admit it. 'I like the kids,' she protested. 'I couldn't leave him to struggle, could I?'

'A lot of people could. Keep in touch, sister mine. And remember you're no good to anyone if your emotional life is wrecked.'

'I'll remember that useful bit of advice,' Lisa said.

It was half past ten before Alex arrived. Lisa knew that the initial stages of meningitis were the most dangerous. If Lucy improved in the first forty-eight hours then things would be easier. But being a knowledgeable doctor wasn't always a good thing. Her heart went out to him when she saw his desolate face. It hadn't quite struck her before what a loving man he was. But she didn't want to show her feelings.

'Lucy's holding her own,' he answered to her query. 'Her temperature spiked earlier but I think that's over now.'

'Good. I promised the kids you'd look in on them when you came home. They'll be asleep but...'

'I'll go to see them. Then I'll have a shower.' A smile showed on his strained face. 'It's good not to come into an empty house.'

When he came down his hair was damp and he was dressed in the old tracksuit she remembered so well. There were dark marks under his eyes. She hid her feelings of sympathy and said, 'Holly made you a salad and there's a steak in the fridge. Shall I grill it for you?'

He looked at her in surprise. 'I'm ravenous and I didn't realise it. But you're not here to cook—you're looking after the kids. I'll do supper.'

'Don't be silly,' she said. 'You look too tired to boil water.'

'I'm too tired to argue. I'd love you to grill me a steak.' From the living room he fetched a bottle and two glasses. 'Malt whisky,' he said. 'I despise men who drink because they think they have troubles. But it looks like I'm joining them.'

'You're entitled to a drink,' she said, 'but not a bottle full.'

'You sound like Lucy. And that's meant as a compliment. Here, I've poured you one.'

She took the offered glass and sipped. She seldom drank spirits—but now she realised what she'd been missing.

'There should be two steaks,' Alex went on. 'Will you have the other yourself? I'd like someone to eat with me. Just for company. You don't have to amuse me or talk to me, just be there.'

'All right,' she said. She recognised the signs of almost intolerable strain in him. Knowing that someone you loved might die was more than most people could cope with. And when that someone had been perfectly well twelve hours before...

After they'd finished their steaks Lisa fetched cheese and biscuits. The colour was coming back into his cheeks so he was feeling better. When he spoke his voice was more confident, and the dead tone had gone.

'First of all, I want to say again, Lisa, how grateful I am to you. I could have managed, but you've made it all so much easier.'

'You'd do the same for me.'

He considered her statement. 'Yes,' he said eventually, 'I think I would. Still, we've got arrangements to make, decisions to take.'

Cutting him off, she said, 'Why don't you go back

to hospital and to bed there?' She knew he'd arranged to stay the night. 'Quite frankly, you don't look capable of deciding anything. I've sorted out school with Mrs Wragg, I'll stay tomorrow night and then it's the weekend. I'll be available whenever you want me.'

Available whenever you want me. The line rang through her head, but he didn't say anything.

'That makes three days,' he said. 'Things will be different then. Lucy will be stable or—'

'She'll be stable,' Lisa asserted. 'Now I'm going to bed. I've made it up in Lucy's room. The kids' clothes are laid out. I'll get them off tomorrow and come into the ward a bit late. You can go back to the hospital.'

'I will. You know, Lisa, Lucy's special to me.'

'My mother was special to me,' she said, hoping he wouldn't hear the bitterness in her voice. 'I know what you're feeling.'

Then she went to bed. He would change again and go back to the hospital. Carefully she passed on the other side of the table from him. She didn't dare to be near him...close enough to touch him...feel his warmth and know that she could offer him some comfort. This was something he'd have to come through on his own.

As she was having to do.

On Saturday afternoon Alex came back early from the hospital. With him was someone she recognised at once, though she'd never met him.

'You're Alex's brother,' she guessed. He was shorter than Alex, and a little plumper, but had the same piercing blue eyes and friendly smile.

Mike Scott said, 'I'm so pleased to meet you, Lisa. I've heard such a lot about you.'

'How's Lucy?'

The two brothers exchanged smiles. 'A great improvement,' Alex said. 'Sir Arthur is as cautious as he ever is, but suspects she might be out of danger. I could take Holly and Jack in to see her tomorrow.'

'They'd like that. Now I'll make you both some coffee then I'll go home.'

'You must want to go home, Lisa, but I'd like you to stay and have a coffee with us if you have time. Mike has to go back in an hour.'

So she stayed for a while. It was interesting to watch Mike and Alex together. They had the same kind of relationship as she had with her sisters, an obvious but uncomplicated love. She liked Mike; she guessed he'd be a good GP.

Later, in the solitude of her own home, Lisa did the few necessary things that had piled up. She thought she'd like the quietness but, in fact, she rather missed the company of Jack and Holly. She was to return to Alex's late that night after the children had spent time with their father. There was a decision she had to make.

At ten that night she found him at the kitchen table, a mug of tea to one side and a pile of papers in front of him. 'Paperwork never disappears,' he greeted her. 'I'm just trying to pay a few bills. And I've got to phone the conference organiser in Seattle, explaining why I can't go now. I was going to fly out tomorrow night.'

'I want to talk to you about that. How long will Lucy be in hospital?'

He shrugged. 'About a week. It's quite handy, really, the school Easter holidays start in a week. Mike's wife is a teacher so I'll send the kids down there for Easter. They all get on very well together.'

'You'd leave Lucy next week but not the kids?'

'That's right.'

Lisa took a breath. 'Why don't you go to Seattle? I'm entitled to a week's leave. I'll take it and look after the kids.'

He looked at her, amazed. 'Why should you?'

'I've got quite fond of them. The time is owed me and I've got nothing planned.'

'You know there's no one I'd rather leave my children with. But I can't take advantage of you any longer.'

'I offered,' she pointed out. 'And I'm a free agent.'

Alex looked at her thoughtfully. 'Let me make a couple of phone calls,' he said, 'then we'll talk about it some more.'

She thought it was a strange thing to do, but waited anyway. When he returned he said, 'If your offer is still open then I'll accept. I've really been looking forward to this conference. I expect to learn a lot. And Holly and Jack will be delighted. But there's one condition.'

'Yes?' she asked suspiciously.

'I want to pay you the going rate. I've just phoned an agency to find out what it is.'

He quoted a rate that sounded ludicrously high to her. It also made her angry. 'I'm not doing this for money,' she snapped, 'and I feel insulted that you should offer it to me. This was something for Jack and Holly and Lucy, if not for you. If you want to pay someone then get someone from the agency.'

He held up his hands placatingly. 'I know that,

Lisa, and the last thing I want to do is insult you. But it's for your own good. And perhaps mine.'

'How can that be?'

He spoke slowly, and she could tell he was picking his words with care. 'You're putting yourself in... danger, staying near me, I know. You feel the same way about me as I feel about you. You know what we both want to do, but you feel you shouldn't. I respect your feelings and I'll stick to the agreement we made. Well, I'll try. But if I pay you it puts you in a strong position. I could try to get you to bed if you were a free agent. But once you become, in effect, an employee there's no way I could take advantage of you. Even if you wanted me to. So I'll pay you. For both our sakes. OK?'

'If you say so,' she grumbled.

I just don't understand him, she thought.

CHAPTER SEVEN

LISA managed to get the week off by some frantic phoning, and because most people on the ward wanted time off in the school holidays.

It was strange to live in Alex's house, looking after his children. It was like becoming an instant mother. There were some things about it that delighted her. About others she wasn't so sure.

Mrs Wragg, the neighbour, had been very good, ferrying Jack and Holly to and from school with her two children, so Lisa said she'd do the school run all week. Every morning she dressed and prepared breakfast for her two charges. Then she picked up Mrs Wragg's children and ran them all to school in her Fiesta. In the afternoons she joined the cluster of mothers outside the school gate. One afternoon she was invited into school to listen to a little concert, and had to tell the headmistress that, no, she wouldn't be able to come in next term for a morning each week.

After two days Mrs Wragg invited her in for an afternoon cup of tea. 'Dr Scott was very lucky in finding you someone like you,' she said, 'but you won't be looking after the children permanently?'

'I couldn't, I'm a sister at Blazes Hospital,' Lisa said. 'I have a full-time job.'

Mrs Wragg thought for a moment. 'So you're very friendly with Dr Scott?'

'He works on my ward. He asked me to do this week because he knew I had some time off.' There

was no way Lisa was going to say that she'd volunteered.

Mrs Wragg pushed over a plate of chocolate biscuits and pressed on with her inquisition. 'I get on
very well with Mrs Scott, but the kids need their own
mother. Or someone her age. Is there any chance of
Dr Scott getting married again?'

'Not that I've heard of,' Lisa answered blandly,
'but I don't see all that much of him outside work.'

Mrs Wragg sighed, realising she wasn't going to
prise any gossip out of Lisa. 'Another cup of tea?'
she asked.

Lisa got to know Jack and Holly better. They were
quite distinct in character. Jack had a sense of humour
remarkably subtle for someone of his age, and Holly
was the essentially practical one, who obviously took
after Lucy.

When she could, Lisa went in to visit Lucy. It was
a shock to visit her own ward as a visitor. She felt
quite disorientated. Lucy realised this.

'How does it feel not to be in charge?' she asked
with a smile.

'I don't like it.' Lisa smiled back. 'I just can't believe that the ward can manage without me. But it
obviously can, and I suppose it annoys me a little.'

'No one is as essential as they think they are,' Lucy
said quietly. 'Things can change, sometimes for the
better.'

Lisa wondered what she meant by that, but decided
not to ask.

'I'm so glad it's you that's looking after the children,' Lucy went on in a stronger voice. 'It stops me
worrying.'

'I'm really enjoying it.' And this was true.

Alex phoned every other night. If he phoned at his early lunchtime in Seattle he caught them just before the children went to bed. It was good to hear his voice, but when he seemed to want to talk to her she firmly told him that he must talk to his children. That was why he had called.

There was another telephone call—from Denise Scott, Mike's wife. Lisa liked the sound of her at once, cheerful, practical, concerned. 'Any problem, just call me,' she said. 'We could cope with the children here, but it's good of you to have them. They need to settle down in their new school.'

'We're enjoying life together.'

'I'll bet you are, they're nice kids. Listen, I've heard a lot about you—is there any chance of you coming over with Alex for a day? Come and look round rural Gloucestershire.'

It was a really tempting offer but she knew she had to refuse it. 'I'm afraid not. Once back on the ward it'll be non-stop work.'

'I can imagine.' From the tone Lisa guessed that Denise didn't altogether believe her explanation. 'Well, the offer's always there. Hope to see you some time.'

After she rang off Lisa felt a little depressed. She would have liked to have seen more of Alex's family.

She had heard that domestic life was supposed to be the enemy of sensuality. It wasn't for her. Sometimes she looked in Alex's bedroom, saw the book he'd lent to Sarah by his bedside, smelled the expensive cologne he used. Downstairs in the little cloakroom hung the old anorak he'd worn when they'd visited Derbyshire, and it, too, had an evocative smell—of moors and rocks and rain. Everything conspired to remind her of him. Then she thought how much she was missing him, and how she couldn't have him anyway.

In bed was the time when she realised most strongly that this was not a good idea. Lucy had a double bed, unlike her own single one. She couldn't easily get to sleep in it. A double bed was made for two. She couldn't get over the fact that she was acting as a mother, and if Alex was with her she could be a wife as well. Such thoughts were stupid! And they hurt.

The week passed, mostly pleasantly, too quickly. The Friday evening before he was due to fly into Manchester Alex phoned and gave her the time and number of his flight, and asked Lisa if she would order him a taxi. She said she would.

However, the children were really looking forward to his return so she decided they would have an outing. It was only thirty miles so she took them in her car to meet him at the airport.

They watched the planes flying in and out, had a hamburger and bought some comics. She felt a pang as she realised this would be the last time they'd be together—she'd got quite close to them both. When she stood behind them, watching them peering towards the arrivals section, she saw one reason why. From behind both of them looked like Alex, and had his distinctive way of walking.

Lisa saw Alex first. He walked through the arrivals door, a heavy bag in one hand and his briefcase in the other. She gasped with the suddenness of it. She hadn't realised just how much she'd missed him. The pain came rushing back. They'd have a couple of hours together with the children. And then she had to go.

The children saw him before he saw them, and ran, shouting, towards him. Lisa saw his surprise, and then the delight spread over his face as he put down his bags and picked them up to kiss them.

'We're two little bundles of joy,' Jack told him.

'We've had a super time with Lisa,' Holly said.

He walked up to her and kissed her on the cheek, a friendly gesture. She could feel the faint roughness of his skin, smell his warmth, saw the faint wrinkles of fatigue at the sides of his eyes. 'It was a lovely idea, coming to meet me,' he said.

She felt inexplicably shy. 'Not very far to come,' she said jerkily, 'and it saved you the cost of a taxi. Did you have a good conference?'

'Excellent. I learned a lot and there's a couple of ideas I'd like to discuss with you and Sir Arthur. I've brought you a set of the notes as well. But I'm glad to be back. It was good of you to look after the children.'

'I was happy to do it. I'm sure the ward will benefit from your trip.'

Why am I talking to him like this? she asked herself. It's not as if we are strangers.

'We'll think about work later. You say Lucy is fine?'

This was easier. 'I've been in to see her several times. She should be discharged any time now. Would you like to call in on her before we go home?'

They were now inserting themselves into her Fiesta. 'I'd like that very much,' he said, 'but it's more work for you.'

'I'm very fond of Lucy.'

She settled herself behind the wheel. Alex was in the passenger seat and there seemed to be an awful lot of him. When she moved the gear lever her arm brushed his side. This was silly! She'd have to stop being so conscious of him.

She took the children to the hospital canteen while Alex went to see his mother. However, he was soon back. His mother had said he looked tired and she'd see enough of him in the days to come. So they went home.

Lisa had prepared a casserole for his late lunch, and when she said she ought to leave he insisted she stay. She was glad to be in his company, though she knew she'd pay for it later.

After the meal there were presents. Each of the children got a lurid baseball jacket, with the name of the San Francisco 49ers inscribed on the back. 'No one else at school has got one like this,' Jack said in a self-satisfied voice that Lisa recognised.

'And here's something for you, Lisa.' Alex offered her a a tiny box. Inside, lying on black satin, was a gold chain with her name in filigree worked on it as a pendant. She was speechless as he took it out and fastened it round her neck. The necklace was beautiful—but didn't he know what the touch of his fingers was doing to her?

'It's lovely...th-thank you,' she muttered.

She told herself she'd have to go. It was no use prolonging the agony, pretending that she had any part of his life now. 'I'd better be getting back to my flat,' she said. 'I have things to do.'

He looked alarmed. 'So soon. But I thought we might—'

'No, Alex. There's nothing for me here now.'

He knew what she meant. 'I'm sorry, Lisa. Anyway, to business. I said I'd pay you and I will.' He took out a cheque book and started to write. 'Who shall I make this payable to?'

That was it, their time together had ended.

Neutrally she said, 'Leave it blank. I'll pick a charity and fill in the name.'

'But there's—'

'That's what I want, Alex. Now, I've got my bags packed upstairs, I think it's time I went.'

This time he didn't try to stop her. She fetched her bags, gave the children each a hug and said, no, she couldn't stay for tea.

'My brother's coming for them tomorrow,' Alex said, 'but we couldn't have managed without you. Thank you again.'

'They're lovely kids. I've enjoyed being with them. Goodbye, Alex.' And she was gone. As she drove back to her little flat, life seemed desolate.

On Monday morning Lisa was back on the ward. She felt happy, knowing that she could immerse herself in her work. There would be a pile of paperwork to get through, new patients to greet and old ones to say hello to. But waiting on her desk was a large, childishly printed envelope, and inside a laboriously written and coloured card. Messages from Jack and Holly thanked her and asked to see her soon. She slipped the card into her desk drawer.

Alex called to see her later in the morning, but briefly. He explained that he, too, had a lot of catching up to do.

'Lucy's being discharged today,' he said, 'but if it's all right with you I'll pick her up later this afternoon.'

'Of course. She's still weak, she needs all the rest she can get. I'll have her ready for you.' Later on she went to talk to the woman she now regarded as her friend.

'Now you're not going to slide out of our lives are you, Lisa?' Lucy asked. 'We all want to see more of you.'

Lisa couldn't help herself. She was tired of pretending. 'I'd love to see more of you and the kids. And being in Alex's company is wonderful, but afterwards it makes me miserable.'

'You're in love with him.' It was more statement than question.

'Of course I am,' Lisa cried fretfully. 'But all he wants is a casual relationship and that won't do for me.'

Lucy reached out to stroke her arm. 'When each of my sons had his eighteenth birthday I decided I would not interfere with his affairs unless I was asked to. I've stuck to that so far, but I would dearly love to interfere now.'

Lisa patted the hand that stroked hers. 'Please don't,' she said. 'It could only make things worse.'

Alex came for his mother just as Lisa finished her shift, and the three of them took the lift and walked out into the car park together. In spite of saying how well she'd been looked after, Lucy was obviously happy to be out. 'It's good to smell the fresh air,' she said.

'And the traffic fumes,' Lisa put in.

As they walked to Alex's car a voice hailed them. Lisa turned and waved—it was Harry Shea. He had phoned at lunchtime and said he was in urgent need of taking Lisa for a quick drink. She had been only too happy to agree. Harry would take her mind off things.

He was dressed in his usual extravagant manner. Today he wore a dark brown suit with nipped waist and padded shoulders. When he caught up with them he picked Lisa up with more than his usual ebullience, and kissed her soundly.

Over his shoulder Lisa saw Alex's face. He frowned disapprovingly. A bleak laugh welled up in her. Alex didn't approve of one of her men friends. Wasn't that sad?

When Harry put her down Lisa introduced him to Alex and Lucy. Alex gave a thin-lipped smile, but Lucy was entranced. Lisa hadn't known that she was an avid fan of Harry's programme. Soon the conversation was solely between Lucy and Harry.

'If you're a friend of Lisa,' Harry said eventually, 'then you must come and look round the set. Meet a couple of the actors. We don't do it often, but I can arrange it.'

Lucy's delight was obvious. 'Could I really? You've no idea how much I'd like that.'

'When would you like to come?'

Alex broke in. 'It's very kind of you, Mr Shea,' he said curtly, 'but my mother's been ill recently and she must rest. Perhaps in a week or two?'

Harry was expansive. 'No trouble at all. Here's my card. Why don't you ring me when you're ready. Like I said, I'd do anything for a friend of Lisa's.'

Alex reached for the card, but Lucy clutched it first. 'I'll keep that,' she said, 'then there's no danger of it getting lost.'

Harry led Lisa away with his arm around her waist.

She glanced back at the glowering Alex, and felt a vindictive pleasure at his discomfiture.

'I like him,' said Harry, when they were sitting in the snug of a little pub quite close to the hospital. 'Trust a man who can't help showing what he's feeling. He tried to hide it, but he didn't like me because he thought I was coming between you and him.'

'He's got no call on me, Harry.'

'I know that. But he certainly wishes he had a call on you.'

Irritated, she said, 'How can you possibly know that?'

'I'm an actor. I study how people behave so I'm convincing when I'm acting.' Harry swallowed some of his tomato juice. 'Are you going to tell him that we really are just good friends?'

'If he's suffering, then let him. So am I.'

Harry squeezed her gently. 'That's not the real you talking, Lisa.'

She decided to change the subject. Harry was being a bit too perceptive. 'Why the sudden invitation, Harry?'

He smiled, a beam of genuine pleasure. 'I'm getting married, Lisa. I wanted you to know early.'

'Married?' she asked, astonished. 'You, getting married? Who to?'

'You mean, which little blonde I've been photographed with has finally managed to grab me?' he asked with a great laugh.

She blushed—it had been what she'd meant. 'Sorry,' she said.

'None of them. I'm going to marry Sally Trent. We've been friends for years. She's a make-up artist at the studio, a bit older than me, a widow with one kid. This is her.'

He showed Lisa a photograph of a pleasant-looking woman. She looks nice, Lisa thought, but she's no glamour girl.

'I'm through with fast women,' Harry went on. 'I want to settle down.'

'You may make one woman happy,' Lisa said pertly, 'but you'll make a dozen journalists miserable.'

'They've had their money's worth out of me,' Harry said cheerfully, 'but now I'm retiring.'

'I'm really happy for you,' Lisa said. 'It's lovely to see friends settle down.'

'I wish you could have some of what I'm feeling, Lisa. But I've an idea it won't be too long before you do.'

'Chance would be a fine thing. When do I get to meet the bride?'

'Soon,' Harry said. 'We're going to have a quiet wedding, it's all she wants. But I want you to be there. You can keep my dad quiet.'

They both laughed.

For a change, next day Lisa managed to get to the hospital canteen for a quick bite at lunchtime. It didn't often happen so when she got the chance she felt entitled to it. In a corner she saw Alex, looking grim. After a moment's hesitation she went over to him.

'From the way you're looking, you're going to shout at anyone who sits here, but may I join you?'

He gave her a weary smile. 'Sorry, Lisa. Please do.'

'Lucy doing well at home? Glad to be back?'

'She misses the children, though they'd certainly overtire her. Yes, she's well, thank you.'

He pushed a forkful of beef around his plate, and then said with false nonchalance, 'I didn't know you had such famous friends—actors on television, no less.'

He's annoyed, she thought. But he's got no right to be. She decided to tease him. 'I like Harry. He takes me out quite often. Don't you think that bald men are sexy?'

He pushed his hand through his own thick hair. 'Since you ask, no,' he said. 'So far I've got a vested interest in disagreeing with you.'

'I think bald men are sexy. And Harry's got a wonderful voice, too. So sort of threatening. Have you seen him on TV?'

'With Lucy sometimes,' Alex said. 'Don't you think he rather overacts?'

'No! I think he's wonderful.' She was enjoying herself, teasing him, but when she looked she could see real hurt in his eyes. And she didn't really want him to think badly of her.

'I'm teasing you, Alex,' she said. 'I'm sorry. I nursed Harry's father some time ago and we got to be friends. In fact, yesterday evening he asked me out to tell me he was getting married.'

'So there's nothing between you? You're not...?' His voice trailed away.

'There's nothing between us. And, whatever you meant to ask, no, we're not. We're good friends. If you get to meet him without preconceptions, I think you'd like him, too.'

'I'm sure I would.' His voice was now brighter, she

noticed. 'I know Lucy wants to meet him when she's well enough.'

'So you're glad I'm not involved with an older man?' she asked.

He sighed. 'You know what I like about you, Lisa, it's your sense of timing. You always wait till a man's down, before kicking him.'

'It's the red hair. It makes us vicious.' She patted his arm. 'But we're still friends. Like I am with Harry.'

He turned his hand over and grasped hers for a moment. 'Being friends means a lot to me,' he said.

There was silence for a moment as they both ate, and then he said, 'I'm glad I saw you. I'm not on the ward this afternoon and I wanted to ask you something. Are you doing anything tonight?'

'No,' she said curiously.

'Would you like to go for a walk along the beach? I think we both need to have a talk.'

She thought for a moment. 'All right, then.'

'Shall I pick you up at your flat—say, around six-ish?'

'That'll be fine.' She wondered if she was doing the right thing.

The afternoon started quietly. Then Brian Barnes walked into her office, carrying a small suitcase. She noted his gloating expression. 'Miss Pinckney is leaving,' he said. 'I've brought her some clothes—will you get her ready?'

Lisa felt like telling him not to be so stupid, but decided it would be the wrong thing to do. Barnes appeared too confident, too certain of himself.

'Miss Pinckney's treatment is far from complete. She's still very ill, she can't possibly leave now.'

'Oh, yes, she can. She can discharge herself at any time. Now, are you going to get her ready?'

He was far more self-assured than usual. She looked at his wetly shining eyes, and wondered which particular drug he was on.

'She'll have to have the consultant's permission,' Lisa improvised. 'She'll need drugs if she's leaving.'

'Get the consultant here, then. Only not that Scott fellow. I'm not talking to him. And she can go when she wants. This is a hospital, not a prison. I should know, I've been in both.'

She decided that sending for Alex might not be a good idea so she phoned Sir Arthur's secretary and explained the situation. Sir Arthur was in his office and would come at once.

'Wait in the waiting room,' she said coldly to Barnes, 'and I'll go and see Miss Pinckney.'

'It's no good trying to make her change her mind,' he jeered after her. 'She wants to come out with me. Here, take her clothes.'

Lisa was angry that Barnes had guessed her intentions. And Marie was in one of her truculent moods, not willing to listen to advice. 'Are they my clothes? Well, you can get out while I get dressed.'

Lisa looked at the thin figure, the still pinched face. 'Marie, you're still very ill. You're getting better but you need to stay here. And if you take any illegal drugs you're likely to kill yourself.'

'What do you know about illegal drugs?' snarled Marie.

'I know a lot. So far this year I've had to lay out four people who died on the ward through drug abuse.' Lisa thought she'd try to shock the girl. 'How d'you think I'd feel, having to wash your dead body and then send you down to the morgue?'

It worked. Marie looked even paler and swayed slightly. Lisa felt a pang of guilt.

'He says he'll leave me if I don't come out,' she muttered. 'He sneaked in last night to tell me. And he's all I've got.'

'But he's killing you!'

'I've felt a lot better recently.'

The door was pushed open and in came Barnes and Sir Arthur.

'Your consultant's here now. He can have a quick word and then we're off. If not, I'm calling the police.'

Sir Arthur glanced at Lisa and shrugged slightly. 'Miss Pinckney, you can, of course, leave when you wish. But I must emphasise that you are still ill and the consequences of you leaving could be very serious indeed.'

Marie took strength from Barnes's presence. 'I want to go,' she said.

'Please sign this release, then.' Sir Arthur gave her a paper to sign.

After Lisa had helped Marie dress, Sir Arthur gave her a letter to her GP, told her how to look after herself and suggested that she might come to his day clinic. Marie nodded. Then, declining help, she and Barnes left.

Lisa and Sir Arthur watched them make their way to the lift.

'You're angry, Lisa,' Sir Arthur said quietly, 'and I suppose you're entitled to be. You've worked hard with that girl.'

'I liked her. I thought we were getting somewhere, making some progress.'

'You should remember that easily a quarter of the patients in this hospital are here, in effect, because of self-inflicted injuries. Tobacco, drink, drugs, poor life-style, too much of the wrong sort of food. And there's little we can do to stop them. We just try to patch them up.'

'What will happen to Marie?'

'You know very well. She'll be back. I only hope it won't be too late.'

When he left the ward Lisa went back to Marie's old room and prepared it for its next inhabitant. Stripping the bed and so on was a job which should have been done by a junior nurse, but she needed to do something physical.

There was only a bleak future for Marie. She knew she was risking her life, but she was doing it because she needed Barnes. Lisa realised that in a sense Barnes needed Marie, too. He wasn't completely de-praved, there was some kind of regard for the girl. They had a relationship.

Marie has a man, Lisa thought, which is more than I've got. Then she got angry at herself at the stupidity of the comparison.

CHAPTER EIGHT

LISA wondered why Alex should want to talk to her. Over the past few weeks he had been good to her, respecting her request to be left alone. She thought that he'd found it hard, just as she'd found it hard. On occasion she had found him looking at her with an expression of sadness, even of loss. It had made her long to go to him, to tell him that she felt the same way. But she hadn't, she couldn't.

At lunchtime she'd teased him, pretending a lightness that she didn't really feel. Being with him brought her so much pleasure, but the pleasure quickly turned to pain. She couldn't have him.

Should she try to stop seeing him—even apply for a job somewhere else? Or should she forget her principles and make do with a temporary relationship? He was lonely, so was she—they could sleep together. No one would know so no one would be hurt.

She wanted to sleep with him with an intensity she found alarming. She had had other boyfriends, of course, and had been quite fond of some of them. But none had ever inspired the sheer physical torment that Alex aroused in her. At night she went to sleep, wishing he was by her.

Even as she thought it, she knew it wasn't for her. She had her principles and she would stick to them, no matter what they cost her in misery.

Lisa had changed into boots and trousers when Alex arrived. Round her neck was his pendant, which she hadn't yet taken off. Even at work she wore it, hidden under her uniform.

'Let's get straight off,' he said, 'and make the most of the light. We've been indoors too long.' He, too, had changed—into sweater, jeans and boots. She thought he looked well.

They drove a mile to the car park on the front, and then set off along the beach. To one side of them were sandhills, on the other was the sea. It was a glorious evening after a warm day. She took pleasure in the acrid smell of the beach and the screams of the darting seagulls overhead.

Soon they had left the busy section of the beach. Most people didn't seem to want to move far from their cars. Apart from a few distant figures, they were alone on a great expanse of sand. There was the low throb of engines, and they watched a heavily laden container ship make its way down-channel and out to sea.

'Sometimes I can hear the sound of ships' engines at night,' she said. 'It's exciting.'

'Would you like to be on a ship like that, Lisa? Going somewhere, anywhere, just to be away from your troubles?'

'You can't run from your troubles,' she said robustly. 'They always follow you and running makes them harder.'

'True. You're tough-minded, Lisa. I've always liked that in you.'

She didn't reply to his odd compliment. Instead she said, 'I like it here. The ranger told me that there are foxes and seals on the waterline at night. They're not seen very often—but they're there.'

'It's surprising how things can survive,' he said, 'how different lives can be.'

She didn't think he was talking about wild animals.

They paced on for another ten minutes in silence and then Alex said, 'I wanted some time alone with you Lisa, some time in which we're not bothered by the hospital or by my family. We don't talk because we don't have the chance.'

She didn't like this. 'Are you going to talk about us—about our relationship? Because I think we've said everything that can be said.'

In a rare moment of irritation he kicked a plastic bottle that rattled over the sand ahead of them. 'I've got to know you well recently, Lisa. There's nobody's company I'd rather have. Do you know what it's doing to me, just being near you and not being able to touch you? It's tearing me apart.'

Her voice was a wail. 'What d'you think it's doing to me? I asked you not to start this conversation. I can work with you only if you don't...don't crowd me.'

'We could have so much, Lisa! It's madness not to do what we both want!'

'I know. To start with, it would be wonderful. You don't know how much I think about you. But it would end and then I'd be desolate.'

'Why should it end?'

'Because I'd just be a part of your life. An important part perhaps, but I wouldn't be everything to you. And when you got a job somewhere else, or met someone new, or maybe just when the passion was dulled...then you'd leave me. True love starts when passion has gone.'

'Or else it doesn't,' he said morosely, and she knew

he was thinking about his own marriage. 'I swore I'd not make the same mistake again, Lisa.'

'And I'm not going to make it at all. You know about my father. You know he's been held by guerillas in South America?'

He bowed his head gravely. She'd confided to him everything that Rosalind had told her, and he'd been supportive, comforting.

'Well, he was left with three little girls to bring up. It wasn't an easy job and he was still a young man. About your age. Three or four years after my mother's death he started seeing a woman at the college he worked at. He brought her home for tea a few times, and we didn't like her. Then she didn't come any more and we were glad—we'd thought she might split the family. Anyway, I asked him when I was much older what had happened to her. He said he'd asked her to marry him—but she wouldn't. She wanted to keep what she called her freedom. She would sleep with him but she wouldn't live with him. So he finished with her. For him a commitment was complete or it was nothing. And I feel the same way. I'm going home now, Alex. You carry on with your walk.'

She turned away, her shoulders heaving. After a hundred paces or so she turned briefly to look at him. He hadn't moved; his figure was stark against the smooth yellow sand. She could see her footprints leading away from him.

The bright spot in the darkest month of her adult life was Harry Shea's wedding. She bought herself a new hat, sat with Harry's dad, Lennie, and thoroughly enjoyed herself.

The ceremony was at a registry office, with about

thirty close friends as guests. Afterwards they went to a hotel for lunch. Sally, the new Mrs Shea—or Mrs Shackleton, to be exact—came and sat next to her. She kissed Lisa on the cheek.

'I'm glad you're here,' she said. 'Harry's told me such a lot about you. I hope you'll carry on going for a drink with him.'

'I like talking to him,' Lisa said. 'He's a very sensitive man.'

Sally laughed. 'He is, you know. But look at him. Who would think it?'

For once Harry had been relatively restrained in his choice of clothes. His dark suit and white shirt were in impeccable taste, but the shaved head and thick moustache still made him look villainous.

'We're going to Scotland for a week,' Sally went on, 'but when we come back you must come round for a meal. Is there anyone you can bring?'

'You mean, a man? No. Not at the moment.'

'That's a pity. I'm so happy I want everyone to be like me.'

Lisa hugged her. 'My chance will come. And now I'm happy for you, too.'

But when she'd waved the newly married couple off on their honeymoon, she wondered when her chance would come. Or if it would.

She was twenty-eight, had a job she liked and did well, had her health, had loving friends and relations. She looked at the patients in her ward without the blessings she had, many keeping cheerful in spite of pain. It was time to stop moping, get herself a life. She despised people who felt sorry for themselves.

A fortnight previously a rather sad Sarah had told

Lisa that after much heavy hinting Paul Evans had finally invited her out to dinner. 'I turned him down, Lisa. I was tempted, of course—I think he's a really nice man. He's improved a lot recently. But he's too young for me. The next man I go out with—if I go out with anyone—will have to be exactly right.'

Lisa knew that her divorce had left Sarah emotionally scarred. She was frightened of forming a new relationship. She wondered if she'd done the right thing.

Then Paul Evans invited her out.

The cardiac consultant was retiring and his department had arranged a dance for him. It was more a party really, in the hospital social club. There would be a formal dinner and presentation later in the month.

Pink-cheeked, Paul asked her if she would like to go as his guest. 'We could have dinner first,' he mumbled, 'then arrive when things are warming up.'

'Paul, I'd love to,' she said. 'It's time I got out and about. And dinner sounds great.'

A vast smile spread across Paul's face. 'I'll pick you up at your flat,' he said.

She was a free agent. She hadn't been to a large affair since the Blazes Ball when she'd first met Alex, and she wanted to forget that.

She went to considerable trouble to dress well. Over a pair of black velvet trousers she wore a black silk blouse. It was long-sleeved and high-necked, but the soft material clung to her figure. She didn't wear the pendant Alex had given her.

When Paul called for her he looked amazed. 'Good Lord, Sister,' he said, 'you look sensational.'

'Not Sister now,' she reminded him gently, 'I'm Lisa.' She looked approvingly at his light grey suit.

He took her to a newly renovated dockland pub for
dinner, where they had a table next to a window, looking out over the river. The meal was well cooked, and
Paul a pleasant companion. She'd got to like him
more and more recently, realising that the brash exterior was just a cover for his innate shyness. Now
that they were outside the narrow confines of the hospital she found out more about him.

He was still a bit gawky. He didn't like it when
the conversation stopped, didn't realise that people
needed occasional silences. Unlike— She made herself not think of Alex.

Finally they saw sailing boats on the river and it
turned out that he had a dinghy. Once she got him
talking about sailing he was quite happy. He invited
her to come crewing for him one day.

Then they went on to the dance. They sat at a table
with another couple, both young doctors. Lisa enjoyed
herself, seeing old friends, dancing, laughing. The retiring consultant made a witty speech and said there
was a bottle of wine to go on every table. There was
a big cheer at this.

It was a good evening, but Lisa felt an odd sense
of detachment, as if she were standing back, conscious
that she was enjoying herself but wondering why. I've
been working too hard, she thought.

She went to the ladies' cloakroom and on her way
back she came face to face with Alex and Lucy. She
was shocked. For some reason she hadn't thought
Alex would come. But why shouldn't he?

Lucy was obviously very pleased to see her, although Alex looked slightly taken aback.

'I've brought Lucy to show her that doctors can
have a good time as well as being serious,' he said.

'You're looking well, Lucy,' Lisa said. 'I'm glad you're recovered. Will I see you and Alex dancing?'

'Possibly,' the older woman said. 'Will you come and join us or are you with a party?'

'I'd love to,' Lisa said, 'but, actually...' At that moment Paul came up to claim her.

There were quick greetings. Paul, of course, had seen Lucy on the ward. Then he led Lisa away, putting his arm round her waist in a proprietorial fashion. Lisa saw a gleam in Alex's eye. She hoped no one else did.

She enjoyed the dance. Once she saw Alex on the floor with Lucy, but then he disappeared. Paul was good company. He pressed her to him while they were dancing, but not too much. She enjoyed the banter between the young doctors, but they *were* young. She'd forgotten how young they were. I'm turning into an old maid, she thought.

They had drunk too much wine so, very sensibly, Paul took her home by taxi. Outside her flat he kissed her. She liked him and hugged him back—she even liked kissing him. But there wasn't that thrill...

He pushed her back gently, but kept hold of her arms. 'There's nothing happening, is there?' he asked. She couldn't see his face, but his voice was both friendly and sad.

'No. I don't think there is. It's a pity, 'cos I like you very much.' She leaned forward to kiss him, but she knew it would be no use.

'We can still be friends,' he said.

'We *are* friends.' She wondered if she was going to wander through life as a woman with many friends but no lover. 'Would you like to come up for coffee?'

'Yes, I'd like that.' As she unlocked the downstairs

door he went on lightly, 'Well, our new understanding will at least save me from the anger of our specialist registrar.'

She looked at him in some surprise. 'What do you mean?'

'He wasn't best pleased at seeing the two of us together. On Monday you'll have to tell him that there's nothing between us, that we're just friends, then he won't scowl at me.'

'You're talking nonsense,' she said amiably. 'Like you, Alex is a friend.'

'Not entirely like me.'

The light was on in her flat. Rosalind was there working. Instantly Lisa was worried. 'It's Dad, isn't it? There's been another message.'

'There has, but it's not bad news. Please introduce me to your friend.'

Lisa hid a smile as she made the introductions. Rosalind was younger, a medical student, but it was Paul who was put off by her coolness and self-possession. She left them talking and went to make coffee.

When she returned with her laden tray she couldn't work out who was instructing whom on medicine. At any rate, they were talking as equals. Lisa realised Rosalind was quoting from the notes from the lecture she'd been to with Alex. She had read them, understood them and looked up the suggested references. Paul, of course, had done the same.

Lisa placed the tray on the coffee-table. 'What's the news about Dad?'

'I got a letter this morning. This was inside.' Rosalind passed her a photograph. Lisa grabbed it. It showed an evil bunch of men gathered in front of a grove of trees. They wore sombreros, were unshaven and most carried guns. But all were grinning broadly. In the middle of them was her father, and the sight of him made her chest tighten. But he, too, was grinning. He appeared quite happy and at ease with the men who had captured him.

'Negotiations have started,' Rosalind said, 'but the guerillas say they won't harm Dad. Apparently, they quite like him. He's teaching them English.'

Lisa shook her head, tears in her eyes. It was typical of her father.

The three of them chatted a while longer and then Paul said he must go. Lisa saw him out of the front door, kissed him again and said, quite sincerely, that she'd enjoyed the evening. Then she went back to her sister.

'He seems quite a nice young man,' Rosalind said, with the air of a fifty-year-old. 'He's promised to send me copies of a couple of papers. Is there anything in it, Lisa?'

Lisa shook her head. 'I like him, but I can't feel anything more than that for him.'

'Because of the other one,' Rosalind said, with her typical shrewdness. 'Come and give me a hug, sister mine.'

CHAPTER NINE

LISA was in her office the following Tuesday afternoon when the phone call came through from
Casualty. 'We've got Marie Pinckney back, Lisa.
She's just been brought in by ambulance. She looks
in a pretty bad way.'

Lisa understood the unspoken message. The girl's
life was in danger. 'Send her up, I've got a bed ready.'
She felt sick—but not really surprised.

'Her parents are here,' the voice went on. 'They
came in the ambulance with her.'

'Parents?' She was surprised. 'I thought she'd lost
touch with them.'

'Well, they're here now. They seem a nice couple.'
The voice was guarded again. 'They're rather upset.'

It wasn't long before the trolley was delivered to
her ward, and the minute she saw Marie's waxen face
Lisa knew there would be little they could do. Marie
Pinckney had overabused her body for the last time.

Trailing behind were a man and woman, aged about
sixty, presumably Marie's parents. Lisa introduced
herself, smiled gently and propelled them towards the
waiting room. 'I'll be along to speak to you as soon
as I can,' she said. Then she sent down the ward for
Paul.

'You'd better bleep Dr Scott,' Paul said, after the
quickest of examinations. 'She's obviously going to
need intensive care.' She knew they shared the same
thought. It wouldn't do much good.

158

Alex came ten minutes later. Wordlessly Lisa handed him Marie's notes and led him to her room. His examination didn't take long either. There could only be one conclusion.

There was no vein in Marie's wasted arm for an IV line so Alex introduced a central venous catheter into her chest to pump in antibiotics and fluids. There was a heart monitor and a catheter into her bladder, but Marie's liver was failing rapidly. There was little that could be done.

To herself, Lisa assessed Marie on the Glasgow coma scale, giving her numbers for eye opening, motor and verbal responses. Marie scored low.

'I'll go and have a word with the parents,' Alex said when there was no more to be done, 'though it's not something I'm looking forward to. Then they can come and sit with her.'

Lisa nodded. 'I'll try and make her look a bit more presentable.' She combed Marie's hair, then quickly washed her face and hands. Alex reappeared with Mr and Mrs Pinckney. 'Any change at all, Sister,' he said, 'bleep me.'

Marie's parents sat by her bed, and Mrs Pinckney took her daughter's hand. 'You've combed her hair, Sister,' she said. 'She looks nice.' This tiny act of kindness seemed to upset her and she started to cry. 'My little girl,' Lisa heard her sob. 'My little girl.'

Lisa left. There was nothing she could do.

An hour later she took them cups of tea. Marie's father followed her out of the room. He seemed to want to talk. Lisa knew that this was a common reaction when people were trying to come to terms with something that had shocked them.

'She keeps on saying "my little girl",' he said,

sounding almost puzzled, 'but Marie's not little any
more. And when we saw that dreadful place she was
living in, Sister... It was filthy. She wasn't brought
up like that, she was always a tidy little girl.'

'Was anyone in the house with her?' Lisa asked
delicately.

'No. Apparently some fellow does live there but he
wasn't in. We banged on the door and it opened so
we went in. She had collapsed on the settee. The room
hadn't been cleaned in months and it smelled! I ran
next door and asked a neighbour to phone an ambulance. I wish...I wish we could have got there earlier.'

'How did you come to call?' Lisa asked. 'I
thought...you hadn't seen her for a while.'

'Neither seen her nor heard from her. In fact, we
thought she was in Birmingham. She'd never tell us
where she was before. Said she had her own life to
lead, and there was nothing we could do. Then last
week she phoned and said she'd like to come home
for a while and visit us, but she had a few things to
do first. She gave us her address. When she didn't
phone back, well, we came over.'

He hesitated, the horror of the meeting obviously
still fresh in his mind. 'When she phoned she said
she'd been in hospital, that a sister there had been
good to her and had told her to get in touch with us.
Would that be you?'

'It might,' Lisa said dully, 'but the nurses and the
doctors were good, too.'

'Well, I'd like you to know how grateful we are.
But I think we've got here too late.' He smiled
wearily, and Lisa's heart went out to him. 'I'm taking
up your time. I'd better go back in.'

You care but you don't get involved, Lisa told herself. She was a professional—she had to walk the line between concern and detachment. But it was hard at times. It sounded as if Marie had taken the first faltering step towards pulling herself out of the morass. She had phoned her parents. And it looked as if it had been too late.

Later she went back into the room and asked the couple where they were staying. They looked surprised at the question. They had travelled from a small town in Derbyshire but had made no plans.

'I know a lot of people use the Elton Hotel,' Lisa suggested. 'It's quite close and it's comfortable. Why don't you book in there and have a meal? You can come back this evening—there's nothing you can do now. I'll phone you if there's any—change.'

The Pinckneys duly departed. The experience was too much for them, they would be guided by anyone.

Lisa went to her room and forced herself to concentrate on her paperwork. Half an hour later the door was thrown open and a voice snarled, 'All right, where is she?'

Lisa had known that Brian Barnes would come, but somehow she had thrust it out of her mind. She turned to look at him in his dirty anorak and jeans, unshaven face and glittering eyes. She knew she should treat him calmly and professionally, but she didn't feel calm and professional. She felt angry.

'One,' she said, 'this is my office so you knock before entering. Two, we have sick people on this ward so kindly keep your voice down. Three, if you have a question, ask it politely and you might get answered. Now, what d'you want?' She was aware that her own voice had risen slightly.

Barnes seemed a bit taken aback by this attack.

'Touchy, aren't you?' he asked. 'You know who I want, Marie Pinckney. They said in Casualty that she'd been brought up here.'

'She has. She's very ill. What drugs have you been pumping into her?'

'Marie is an addict, she can't help herself. She's got to have drugs.'

'She could help herself if she had friends who'd support her,' Lisa snapped. 'I'm afraid you can't see her—she's in Intensive Care. Only her next of kin can see her.'

'I'm next of kin, aren't I?'

'You are not. Her parents are. They're here now and I'm sure they don't want her to have anything more to do with you.'

'She lives with me and I've got a right to see her!' Barnes lurched forward, spittle spraying from his lips.

Lisa didn't move, but faced him down. Just for once she couldn't help herself. 'You want to see her before she dies?' she asked brutally.

It seemed to get through to him. 'She's not going to die,' he scoffed, but there was doubt in his voice.

'It seems very likely that she is.'

Now she saw fear, panic even, in his eyes. 'You're just having me on, trying to scare me.'

'I wish I was, but I'm not.'

'Well, I'm going to see her and you're not going to—' He moved towards her and for a moment she thought he was going to attack her.

Then the door opened behind them and a voice rasped, 'You—outside.'

It was Alex, and she'd never been so pleased to see him. But he was not the normal, calm doctor that she knew. His face was white and there was an expression in his eyes that was terrifying. She remembered the saying, 'Beware the anger of a quiet man.'

Even Barnes seemed to realise that this was not a good time to be awkward. 'I just want to see Marie Pinckney,' he mumbled.

'You can't. Now get off this ward and out of this hospital. If I see you here again Security will hold you until the police cart you away.'

'You can't do that! I've got rights and—'

'Marie Pinckney had rights,' Alex hissed. 'She had the right to live. You took it from her. Now get out!'

The two faced each other, but it was no contest. Barnes moved away. At the door he turned and with feeble defiance said, 'I want to know how she is. And I'm holding you responsible, you're the doctor.'

Alex didn't answer, and Lisa saw the fear growing in Barnes's eyes.

'You can phone me here,' she said. 'I'll tell you how she is.' Barnes left.

'I'll follow him to the lift,' Alex said.

She was slumped in her chair when he returned. 'You need a hot drink with plenty of sugar,' he said. 'Just like before.' She nodded.

He made her the drink and then sat close by her. 'I was listening outside. Your tough side was coming out again.'

Lifelessly she said, 'I told you I used to work in Casualty. You have to be tough there. Has he gone?'

'He has, but I'm not certain he won't be back.'

'There's genuine feeling there somewhere,' Lisa said. 'It's just got through to him that she really might die. And he doesn't know what to do.'

'Addicts hate it when one of their number tries to break away. That's why he took her off the ward. He

needed her in his power. Now he's trying to sort out
the idea that he's responsible for her death.'

'Yet I'm sure he loves her,' Lisa said. 'Funny kind
of love.'

'Love takes a lot of different forms.'

'Don't I just know it,' she muttered, half to herself.

Now she could feel her heartbeat slowing and felt
calmer. She looked at Alex and he, too, seemed more
tranquil than he had been. The terrible cold rage had
left him.

'Fine doctor and nurse we are,' she said. 'What
happened to professionalism? We're supposed to be
detached, passionless.'

'Even doctors and nurses are entitled to some feelings,' he said. 'Now, I've got something else to trouble you with. Perhaps it's the wrong time to ask, but
I promised I would so I will.'

'I'm on call all weekend and Mike's coming to pick
Lucy up. He's bringing the kids up for the ride. They
asked me to ask you that if they were at home would
you come and stay with them on Saturday night? I
could run them down next week. I told them it was
an imposition and that you had things to do, perhaps
friends to see. They understand that, but said if you
had nothing on would you think about it?'

'What about you?' she asked.

He understood the point of her question at once.
Wryly he said, 'You wouldn't see me. I'm staying
here all weekend. I've borrowed a room again for a
couple of nights.'

But I want to see you, she thought, then pushed the
thought down. Looking at him, she recognised that he
knew what she was feeling.

He went on expressionlessly, 'I thought you might

be going out with young Paul again. Did you enjoy the dance last week?'

There was no point in trying to deceive him. 'I like Paul very much and I enjoyed the dance, but I doubt if I'll be going out with him again.'

He looked at her, his blue eyes questioning.

'It just didn't work,' she said. 'There was nothing there for me.'

'Is that my fault?'

'Mostly it's mine. If I have principles I must expect to suffer for them. Incidentally, don't be hard on Paul. He knows you've got some kind of—feeling for me.'

He was surprised at this. 'I didn't realise it was so obvious. I thought we had been discreet.'

'He's learning to observe. In time he'll be a very good doctor. Good at diagnosing.'

'Thanks,' he said cheerfully. 'That makes me sound like a disease.'

'Sometimes you act on me like one.' After pausing, she said, 'I'd like to look after the kids. I'll be at your house about ten, shall I?'

'That'll be fine. I'll be there but I'll be straight off to the hospital.'

She looked at the pain in his blue eyes. 'That will be best,' she said.

Mike didn't come to pick up Lucy on Saturday morning—his wife Denise did. Lisa had spoken to Denise briefly on the phone and had liked her. Now she met her in person she liked her even more. She was short and blonde, with an air of efficiency belied by a mischievous smile.

'I'm having a coffee before we set off,' she told

Lisa cheerfully, 'and Lucy's cleaning the kitchen so you don't realise she's a scruffy housewife.'

'I heard that,' came a voice from the kitchen. 'When I get to your house I shall rub my finger along your mantelpiece.'

'Bring a duster, then. Is there a coffee for Lisa?'

The three sat in the kitchen. Denise and her mother-in-law were obviously very fond of each other, and Lisa thought how she'd like to be part of a tight family group like this. Then Lucy went upstairs to fetch her bag, and Denise moved nearer to Lisa.

'It's really good to meet you in person at last,' she said. 'You know how grateful we all are for what you did for Lucy and the family.'

'I like them all,' said Lisa sincerely, 'and I didn't do anything special.'

'You stopped Mike and Alex worrying so much. That was special. Now, are you sure you can't get down to meet my brood some time? Get Alex to bring you.'

There was nothing Lisa would have liked more, but she said, 'Well, I'm kept quite busy, you know.'

The look that Denise gave her was speculative. 'I'm sure you could if you tried. You're good for Alex, you know. He smiles a lot when he talks about you. You're not like that cold bitch in America.'

Lisa blinked then smiled. 'Do you always say what you think?' she asked.

'Too often, I'm afraid. I work in a school for kids with special needs. Some of the parents want picking up and *shaking*.'

Alex came into the kitchen with Jack and Holly. He'd just taken them to the supermarket to select the food they wanted for the weekend. It was time for goodbyes. Lucy kissed her and said there was no one she'd rather leave the children with. Alex didn't kiss her, but left her his hospital number and told her to call if she needed anything. Denise said Lisa had to visit Gloucestershire. Then she was alone with Holly and Jack, and though she loved them she felt a great sense of apprehension. The family seemed to be conspiring to pull her, gently but firmly, towards what? She didn't seem to be in control of her own life. And she didn't like the feeling.

She started the children on a cutting-out game she'd brought, and poured herself another cup of coffee.

It was decision time. She had to face up to it, there was no way she could carry on like this. There was no way she and Alex could simply remain friends. Every time she looked at him, every time she heard his voice, her body reacted to him. She loved him. And she knew that in time she'd give way, not to him but to her own desires.

There was only one thing for it. She would put in her resignation, look for another job, perhaps even go abroad. She could stay with her sister, Emily, for a while. Whatever she did, she had to get out of this half-life, alternating periods of misery with periods of guilty elation.

It wasn't just Alex who was the problem. She'd fallen for all of his family—Lucy, Mike, Denise, Holly and Jack. And she knew that in time, if she gave them chance, all of them would get on with her own family—her father and two sisters.

She just couldn't stand it, she'd have to cut and run. She'd start her search through the nursing press at once.

This is going to make my weekend a fun one, she thought.

Alex sat in a tiny study bedroom in the hospital residence, his eyes skimming the article in front of him for the fourth time. It was no good, his brain just wouldn't function.

He had a topic to research and had borrowed books and papers from the university library. He had allocated this weekend to do the preliminary reading. And his brain wouldn't work. That was odd. He'd never had trouble studying before.

He kept remembering the sharp words whispered to him by his sister-in-law just before she'd left. 'I think she's wonderful. If you don't grab her quickly someone else will.'

He had whispered back, 'I've been married once. I'm not sure I want to repeat the experience.'

'Don't be stupid! You'll never meet another woman like Lisa. Just don't take no for an answer.'

Perhaps Denise saw things a little too simply. Everything to her was black and white. And he had to respect Lisa for the stand she was taking. He wondered where he'd gone wrong—was it his fault? Could it happen again?

No, it couldn't. He *knew* he'd be happy with Lisa. His hand crept to the phone and lifted the handset. Then he replaced it. He was to be a friend, a colleague, but that was all. One of the things that he liked about Lisa was her toughness, even though it made life a bit awkward at times.

His bleeper went. He checked the number then phoned Ward 28. 'You asked to be called about Marie Pinckney,' the staff nurse said. 'Well, she's very yellow now and her pulse is rapid and shallow. She's just vomited and—'

'I'll be right there. Are her parents with her?'

He'd known the end was inevitable. For a while this morning she'd come out of her coma, and he liked to think that she'd recognised her parents. She'd muttered 'Mum' and 'Dad'. Perhaps there had been the chance of some kind of goodbye. The end was now very near.

Alex went on the ward and one glance was sufficient. 'You know what's happening?' he quietly asked the parents.

It was the mother who replied. 'Yes, thank you, Doctor. I think we're expecting it.'

'I think you'd better wait in the waiting room.' Half an hour later Marie's body gave up its unequal struggle. Alex sent the parents back to their hotel. There were arrangements to be made.

It wasn't a good time for Brian Barnes to arrive. He hadn't been back so far. He had phoned and been told officially that Marie's condition was critical. He swaggered down the ward, full of confidence. Alex saw him and wondered what drug he had been taking. Instead of showing the lethargy often produced by heroin, Barnes seemed to be alert, aggressive even. Some kind of stimulant, Alex guessed. Possibly Barnes had been injecting amphetamines. Whatever it was, he'd had too much.

Alex disliked the man intensely, but he was a doctor. Barnes was ill, needed treatment. He knew it was pointless but he had to say something.

'You don't look well, Mr Barnes. I think you need medical assistance. Would you like to tell me what you've been taking?'

'Don't worry about me, Doc, I can look after myself. How's Marie?'

They were in the middle of the ward. Alex walked
towards the office saying, 'You'd better come in
here.'

Barnes had to follow. Once in the office Alex shut
the door and then said, 'There's no easy way of saying
this. I'm sorry, but Marie is dead.'

'Dead? She can't be. You're playing tricks on me.'
Alex could hear the disbelief in his voice.

'It is not a thing I joke about. We did try to warn
you, Mr Barnes, that she had little chance.' Alex's
voice hardened. 'The hepatitis was dangerous. Had
she stayed in hospital she should have recovered. By
leaving hospital...' Alex shrugged.

Barnes had gone white and swayed slightly. His
mouth moved but no sound came out. Alex realised
he was seriously shocked. As Lisa had said through-
out their troubles with the wretched man, there was
some genuine feeling for his partner.

When he did manage to speak Barnes's voice was
almost a shriek. 'I want to see her! You killed her.
This is supposed to be a hospital, isn't it. Why didn't
you cure her?'

The office door opened and the staff nurse looked
in, alarmed. 'Phone security, will you?' Alex asked
quietly.

'Mr Barnes, you can't see her now. The nurses are
preparing her.'

'You let her die just because she was a drug addict!'

This time there was an actual attack on Alex, but
not a successful one. A thin fist caught him on the
cheek but there was no power behind it. With a mix-

ture of distaste and pity Alex wrapped his powerful arms round the man and lifted him off his feet. Barnes tried to kick, to escape, but there was no strength left in the wasted muscles. After the initial spasm he fell limp. A moment later two security guards arrived and took an arm each.

'Shall we call the police, sir?'

Alex shook his head. 'I'm not hurt. When he's quietened down see him off the premises. Try to tell him that he ought to see a doctor. I think he's ill.' They'll love me in Casualty for suggesting that, he thought.

Five minutes later there was a call from Security. 'He did a runner, sir, but we didn't follow. Shouted that he'd get you.'

'You did right.'

It wasn't a pleasant way to spend his time on the ward. He went to chat to the staff nurse in charge and to check that nobody had been upset by the noise. Then he went back to his room.

Still he couldn't work. For a moment he thought of phoning Lisa. He knew she'd taken an interest in Marie. Then he decided not to. She had enough misery, without him adding to it. Besides, he really only wanted to phone her to hear her voice. And that wasn't fair.

What should he do about her? He now knew that he loved her, that he felt a passion deeper than he'd ever felt before. She excited him as no other woman had ever done. On the few occasions he'd touched her he'd felt a charge like lightning between them. When he'd kissed her he'd wanted to do nothing but that all of his life. Undressing her had suggested delights he

could only dream of. To his dying day he would remember the sight of her naked body in the firelight.

But she was more than just an exciting woman. He
had seen her at work, seen her with his children, with
his mother. Lisa would be a perfect companion. She'd
be the perfect wife for a consultant. But was it too
late?

He grabbed the paper on his desk and forced himself to read it. He was here to study.

Through sheer effort of will he managed to get en-
grossed. He read steadily through the hours, taking
notes and marking passages for rereading. It was past
nine when his phone rang—probably some emergency
on the ward, he thought. But it wasn't.

An anxious switchboard operator asked him if he
would accept a call from a Mr Brian Barnes. 'He
sounds very peculiar,' the operator said doubtfully,
'but he says he's got a very important message for
you personally. No one else will do. Shall I route it
to Security?'

'No, I'll take it.' Alex sighed. 'Yes, Mr Barnes?'

The voice was different again, and Alex felt the
faintest twinge of alarm. Barnes sounded even more
confident and vainglorious. Alex knew he must have
had a very large dose of something to bring him so
high again so quickly.

'I've fixed you now, Mr Clever-Dick Doctor. Think
I'm rubbish, do you?'

'I don't think any human being is rubbish,' Alex
said evenly.

'Well, I'm not. Marie was all the family I had and
you took her away. It was your fault she died—you
killed her.' Barnes's voice rose in a crescendo.

Alex realised that Barnes was in a very bad state.

He spoke with utter conviction, and the mixture of delusions and paranoia could be dangerous. Trying to be gentle, he said, 'Why don't you come in for a while? I could arrange for you to see her if you wished. I know you're upset but—'

'I said she was all I had, all my family. Well, I fixed your family, Doctor. Fair exchange—a family for a family. It was easy to find out where you lived.'

Terror gripped Alex but he tried to keep calm. 'I'm at the hospital now, Mr Barnes. What are you—'

'I asked a nurse where you lived, told her I had something to deliver. A family for a family, Doctor.'

'Look, why don't you—?' But Barnes had rung off.

Alex forced himself to think. He rang the police, explained what had happened and then rushed to the darkness of the car park.

He drove home fast, cutting through red lights, his horn blaring. Halfway home he heard the clanging of a fire engine in the distance. The sweat sprang out on his forehead and around the line of his jaw. When he neared home he saw the glow in the sky. He knew what it was but he prayed he was wrong. Let it not be his house, not his children, not Lisa. He didn't want it to be anyone else, but…but it was a fire in his street.

He just had time to tell himself that if they were all right he would do things differently in future. He'd make changes. Then he turned the last corner and there was his house, ablaze.

There were police cars, two fire engines, firemen with hoses. There were even spectators. He leaped out of the car and ran towards the house. A fireman caught him. 'That's my house,' Alex gasped. 'My children are inside.'

'Don't do anything stupid, sir, you'll only hinder our work. Now, how many people were in there?'

Alex forced himself to think. 'A nurse—a friend of mine—and my two children.'

'Three people. Are you sure that's all?'

'I'm sure. Now can I—?'

'Just wait here, sir, and I'll see what I can find out.' The fireman waved to a policeman. 'I'll be back with any news.'

CHAPTER TEN

LISA had enjoyed putting the children to bed. After their bath they had romped a while and then Lisa had kicked off her slippers, got into bed between them and read them a story. They'd had a full day and soon their eyes were drooping so she left them to sleep.

Downstairs, life wasn't so much fun. There was nothing on television and she couldn't bring herself to read. Her thoughts went round and round in a monotonous circle. What was she doing here? She couldn't carry on like this, being just part of Alex's life. She wanted to be at his life's centre or be no part at all. She'd decided to leave. There was a certain bleak satisfaction in having reached a decision. And she was sitting on the same couch where they'd so nearly made love.

The street, the house, were quiet. Too much emotion was tiring and she must have dozed off. She awoke, blinking, uncertain as to what had disturbed her. She'd heard some kind of noise.

There it was again, a scratching sound from the hall. Then a definite snap as the letter-box slammed shut. Perhaps it was a note or a circular. She went towards the hall.

The minute she opened the door she knew something was wrong. It took a while to comprehend as she was still fuddled from sleep. The entire hall stank...of petrol? As she looked she saw the rugs drenched with it, a dark stain creeping across the parquet floor. Then the letter-box opened again.

She watched, paralysed, as a flaming rag was pushed through. It fell on the floor and there was the 'woof' sound of igniting petrol. Instantly the hall was a sea of flames. She could smell her own burning hair before she realised that her face hurt, too.

An indoor fire, her very own nightmare. She couldn't move, a whimper forcing itself through her clenched teeth. Everything was burning, and she was terrified.

There was something obscene about the way the fire was leaping up the walls, blackening the wallpaper, taking hold of the old-fashioned wooden stairs. She was burning. She forced herself to move, to slam the door against the heat. Then she leaned against it, trembling. It wasn't a nightmare, it was real. The house was on fire. She had to run, to escape.

It took more strength than she'd known she had to force down her panic, pick up the phone and dial 999. The matter-of-fact tone of the operator steadied her. This was how she must be, a professional.

'There is a very dangerous house fire at 29 Fareham Grove,' she said clearly, 'and there are two children in the house. Please hurry.'

The operator made her repeat the address and then she rang off.

She must be professional! She must think. The children were upstairs. She tried to open the door into the hall. The doorknob was already hot. Grasping it with her handkerchief, she opened it and peered through. It was an inferno—no one could walk through it. And the children were upstairs!

It was easy enough to open a window and climb

out. She ran round the back to the verandah, where she remembered seeing a ladder. Dragging it round to the side of the house, she propped it against the wall by the large window she knew was at the end of the upstairs corridor. Then she ran back to fetch one of the plastic garden chairs.

She carried it up the ladder and tried to smash it through the window but the glass wouldn't break. Sobbing with fear and frustration, she hammered again and again. 'Come on, break!' she ranted at it through her tears. Finally it did break. A lick of greasy smoke puffed out at her and she could see the dull glow of flames.

She smashed at the projecting fragments of glass, then in desperation dragged down the curtains and bundled them over the bottom sill. Then she rolled into the corridor.

She coughed as she'd never coughed before, her lungs aching with pain. The corridor was full of choking smoke. From somewhere she remembered a lecture she'd once attended. She dropped to the floor—and there was a clear smokeless space about eighteen inches high.

She wriggled along it until she was outside the children's room, scrabbled upwards for the handle and rolled inside. The children were asleep, and so far there was little smoke in the room. She went to the windows first—and could have wept. They had been fitted with child safety bars. No one could get through.

Now there was more smoke in the room, and outside she could hear an ominous crackling. Reminding herself that she must keep calm, she woke the children and crammed them into their dressing-gowns. She mustn't panic them.

'Is this an adventure?' Holly asked. 'I've never had a real adventure.'

'Well, you're having one now,' Lisa said.

There was a washbasin in the corner of the room, and Lisa ladled handfuls of water over all of them. Then she told Holly to stay by her side, and tucked Jack under her arm.

When she opened the door there was a blast of heat and smoke. The fire had got worse. Jack whimpered. 'Don't be silly,' she snapped at him. 'Things are going to be perfectly all right. Now, just wriggle, like me.'

There was heat, flames, smoke. She wanted to leap to her feet and run. But instead she inched her way along the floor, talking calmly to the two children under her charge. But her nerve was going. How long was this corridor? Perhaps they were lost in the dark! The three of them eventually reached the end of the corridor, the smoke eddying above them. Lisa put an arm over the sill, and was aware of a blinding light.

A voice said, 'Shall I take those two?' Jack and Holly were hoisted away. 'Now, then, is there anyone else in the house?'

'Only me,' she quavered.

'You're absolutely certain?'

'Yes, I'm certain.' Strong arms helped her over the sill, and supported her as she stumbled down the ladder.

It was a different scene as she was led away by a fireman. There were two fire engines, their hoses playing on the flames. Where had they come from? And the house was ablaze. As she turned and looked she saw flames bursting out of the window she'd just climbed through.

She could see Holly and Jack, being hugged by their father. Now he was holding them and walking towards her, and she couldn't tell what he was thinking. She wanted to tell him it wasn't her fault.

Suddenly she felt tired. She became aware that her hands and knees were cut, her face was burnt and her lungs ached from the swallowed smoke. A tiny corner of her brain registered what was happening. She'd been running on adrenaline, the fight or flight syndrome. Now the danger was over, and she was likely to... For the first time in Lisa's life she fainted.

She was glad to hand over responsibility to somebody else. She didn't want to think, just nurse her pain. Vaguely she was aware of expert but kindly hands, lifting her onto a trolley and slotting her into an ambulance, and then she heard the roar of the engine and the sound of the siren.

It felt wrong to be taken to her own casualty department. She had felt the same when she'd been taken in to Casualty in Shropshire. She knew a couple of the nurses and the doctor who looked at her. She should be helping, not lying here.

But they were good to her. A nurse helped her undress, her cuts and burns were treated and she was taken to a bed. 'Are the kids all right?' she asked anxiously.

'Perfectly all right. We've had a good look at them but we're not even keeping them in. Dr Scott has taken them to Sir Arthur's house. His housekeeper has offered to look after them overnight.'

She was carefully eased into bed. 'Dr Scott left a message for you. He says he'll be back. There's a policeman here too, but I'll send him away. You can give a statement in the morning. Sleep's the best thing for you.'

She'd been given a sedative and felt sleep closing in on her. But there were things to consider; she felt she had a new insight on something—what was it? Her exhausted body betrayed her and she had to sleep. Just as she drifted off she was dimly aware of the door to her little room opening and someone gently stroking her bandaged hand. Perhaps they were taking her pulse again.

Waking was a painful process. Something told Lisa it would be better to stay asleep—but she couldn't.

She wasn't muddled about what had happened. Every detail of the fire was fixed in her mind with painful clarity. The odd thing was that she didn't have that sick feeling of terror she'd had in the past. Somehow she'd overcome her fear of fire.

But she hurt. Her knees hurt, her hands hurt, her face and neck hurt, her lungs felt as if they had been sandpapered. And she smelled of smoke. Her hair had burned, she could tell.

A nurse came in with tea, but she had to sit and feed it to Lisa. Then Lisa asked her for a mirror. 'Oh, my God,' she gasped. She looked terrible! The nurse trimmed off some of her burned hair and lent her a pretty scarf to put round what was left. Then her friend Mike Gee, the casualty consultant, came in to examine her. The young doctor she'd seen the night before hovered tentatively behind him.

'Since it was you, I came in person,' he said. 'We medical staff have to hang together. Now, let's have a look.'

His examination was deft and thorough. 'Painful

GILL SANDERSON 181

but superficial,' he said finally. 'You won't need to trouble our burns unit. You can go home later but stay off work for a week.'

'I've never been off work sick in my life,' she said, 'and I'm not going to start now.'

'You'll have to. You've had quite a shock. And you'd only frighten the patients like that. Incidentally, you've got a visitor. Been here quite a while.'

He left. And in came Rosalind. Lisa felt a tiny twinge of disappointment—and then felt guilty. She'd hoped it would be Alex.

Rosalind was cool as ever but Lisa could detect a thread of emotion under her careless words and even the glisten of a tear in those dispassionate silver eyes.

'You're a hero—or a heroine, sister mine,' she said with some amusement. 'Your name will be in the local paper tomorrow night.'

'I don't feel heroic now.'

'You don't look it either.' Rosalind sat on the bed. 'Is there any part of you I can hug?'

'Sort of below my arms,' Lisa said. 'Just keep away from my hands and face.'

Rosalind gently put her arms round her and leaned her head on Lisa's breast. As she looked down, Lisa remembered the times she had nursed her as a baby. There was a tremor in Rosalind's voice as she released her. 'I've only got two big sisters,' she said. 'I couldn't spare one, you know.'

Lisa knew that for Rosalind this was a very passionate speech, but when she sat by the bed she was her old remote self. 'Do you feel as rough as you look?'

'Worse, probably. Er, d'you know how Alex's children are?'

'The ones you pulled out of the fire? Both doing fine. No ill-effects at all. Apparently, their father came back here last night but you were already asleep.'

'Oh,' said Lisa. She remembered the hand stroking hers. She wished she'd been awake.

'Now the good news. I've got a letter from Dad— it's to all of us. Not just a message, a real letter.' She fumbled in her bag.

'Is he free? Have they released him?'

'No, the guerillas are still holding him, but he seems cheerful enough.'

It was a long letter, written on pages torn out of a child's school book. It was like the letters she'd received so often before—chatty, concerned, observant. He told them all not to worry—and she was quite sure it had not been written under duress. He wasn't free but he was all right. The relief she felt made her pains seem trivial.

The nurse popped her head round the door. 'Another visitor?' Lisa nodded.

Alex came in. They looked at each other for what seemed like endless minutes. He was dressed in a white shirt and dark trousers. There were worry lines around his eyes and his forehead was wrinkled. She could guess what he'd been through. Even the thought of your children dying was terrifying.

Eventually Lisa said, 'Alex, this is my sister, Rosalind. Rosalind, this is Dr Scott—Alex.' She couldn't think what to say so she took refuge in formality.

Calmly, Rosalind said, 'So you're the man who's making my sister's life a misery?'

He replied with equal calmness, 'No. I'm the man who loves her and will do anything for her.'

There was a silence as Rosalind considered this, then she said, 'Well, that's all right, then. Nice to meet you, Alex. I expect I'll be seeing more of you. Lisa, if you're going home tonight I'll come and spend a couple of nights with you.' She left.

Lisa winced, which was painful. She said, 'Sorry about my sister. She never graduated from charm school.'

Alex shook his head absently. 'I like ruthless honesty. Just think how much simpler medicine would be if patients always told us the exact truth.'

'Much simpler.' The conversation was dismaying her. They seemed like two casual acquaintances or even a doctor and patient. He didn't see her like that, did he? Her mouth turned down when she realised how he did see her—she looked a mess.

He was continuing in the same matter-of-fact way. 'I'm afraid there are going to be questions from the police, and even a reporter. I'll try to keep them away for a while. The man who started the fire has been picked up. It was Brian Barnes. He's now in hospital—he took a massive overdose. I doubt he'll survive.'

Lisa guessed the rest. 'Marie died?'

'I'm afraid so. You were right, in his own twisted way he really did love her.'

Alex paused. His gaze fastened on her throat. Last night she'd been wearing the pendant he'd given her. On her inflamed skin he could see the line of the chain, the mark where her name had been. He shuddered.

'You saved the lives of my children last night, Lisa. And I know how you feel about fire. It must have taken strength I can only dream of for you to do what you did. But you did it.'

She tried to shrug. 'I'm a nurse,' she said. 'We try to save lives. And you'd have done the same. Anyway, the fire brigade would have got them out.'

'Perhaps. But you did.' He frowned, then he burst out, 'Lisa, what's wrong? We're here talking like two polite strangers. Last night, for one dreadful half-hour, I thought everything good in my life was gone. And now…now I can't even hold you or kiss you.'

She stretched her bandaged hands towards him. She said, 'My family hug a lot. Rosalind just hugged me. If you keep away from my hands and my face, well, the rest of me's all right.'

He eased himself onto the bed and with infinite care wrapped his arms round her. She rested her arms on his shoulders. 'I can't hug you,' she whispered, 'but I want to.'

His head was resting on her breasts, as Rosalind's had done. But it produced a wildly different set of feelings. His arms tightened around her. She could sense the passion in them but knew he was being gentle with her. 'You can hold me tighter than that,' she said.

He did. The top two buttons of her blue hospital issue pyjamas had come undone. He bent his head to the swell of her breasts and another button popped open. She lay there as gently he kissed her soft pink peaks, now erect and demanding. She wanted to lie there for ever.

'I like that,' she said plaintively when he stopped.

'So do I,' he growled, 'but we have things to decide first.' Carefully he rebuttoned her pyjama jacket.

'Last night,' he said, 'I thought my children might

be dead and there was nothing I could do about it. You can guess how I felt.'

She nodded. His torment had been worse than hers. At least there had been something she could try to do.

'I thought you might be dead too, and my despair doubled. I realised then that life without you was insupportable. I've been too, too careful! It's obvious that I love you and I want to marry you and I will! Even if you move, I'll follow you. Life's too short, too precious. You know we're made for each other. So marry me!'

The silence between them stretched on and on. He was staring at her, his blue eyes blazing, his lips taut. She remembered again—'beware the anger of a quiet man'.

'All right, I'll marry you,' she said. 'I can't imagine anyone I'd rather marry, I've loved you since I first met you and I love you more now. But don't think I'm marrying you because you shouted at me!'

'My darling!' He couldn't throw himself into her arms. Instead, with infinite delicacy, he leaned forward and brushed her lips with his.

'I must taste awful,' she said. 'And I know I look awful. But I feel so good.'

He sat on the bed again, his arm around her waist. 'You're as happy as me,' he said. It was more a statement than a question.

'Yes. The same thing happened to me last night. At one stage I thought I might die. And it wasn't my life that flashed before my eyes, it was what I hadn't done with my life. It was regrets for chances missed. And what I hadn't done was…well, you know, with you. I decided that if I got out I would.'

'Don't you want to wait until we're married?' he asked mischievously.

'No. Like you said, life is too short. And today is the first day of the rest of our lives...'